The Question of LAHASH

THE Question of LAHASH

Nicole Mayor

4-U-Nique Publishing

Breaking the Status Quo, One Book at a Time.™

4-U-Nique Publishing

A Series of VLB/VBJ Enterprises, LLC

4-U-Nique Publishing books may be purchased for educational, business, or sales promotional use. For information, please email: info@4-U-Nique Publishing.com

Second Edition

Cover Design By: 4-U-NiquePublishing

Library of Congress Cataloging-in-Publication Data

ISBN-13: 978-0692155974

ISBN-10: 069215597X

Acknowledgments

I want to thank my husband, George, for his input throughout the writing process, as well as my children, whose encouragement helped get me to the finish line.

1

$\mathcal{T}$he alarm clock sounded at 6:00 a.m. It had always been a touch-less torture to Kate, even in her days in the military when waking at the crack of dawn was the norm. These days, she relished any morning that she didn't have to hear that blasted *beep beep beep beep!* The high-pitched relentless call to pull her from a deep sleep, while hugged on either side by her pillow soft mattress and warm down comforter, was enough to keep her in a semi-bad mood half the morning. Today was no different.

After two snoozes of the alarm, she finally managed to drag herself out of bed and break the delirium with a hot shower. As she went through her morning routine, a silent debate raged in her mind.

I should just quit. This job is getting me nowhere, and the though of another boring interview that adds nothing to a single person's understanding of the world, of life, of anything is just a waste of time. Why do I do it?

Because if I didn't do it, how else would I pay my bills? Get married and let a man take care of me? Ha! I haven't met a man worth the effort to change all my bad habits—at least not one who is available.

Despite Kate's lack of enthusiasm now for her job as a celebrity gossip writer, she was thrilled when they had hired her three years ago. She was twenty-seven at the time and had just finished two tours in the air force and her final year of college. She called it her eight-year vacation because she had taken advantage of the time living overseas to travel around Europe and other Mediterranean countries, Israel and the Middle East, and a few jaunts to Japan and other islands.

Traveling can spark a creative nerve in a person and make them seek out ways of expressing that creativity. In Kate's case, this manifested itself in a daily ritual of journaling that often had nothing to do with her own personal life. Rather, she typically analyzed current events or theorized about the lives of famous people she hadn't met. The change in diplomatic relations between the US and Cuba, for example, filled at least six pages in her journal. She actually conducted research before expressing her opinion in her journal; just in case someone in the future ever read it, they would be impressed by her knowledge of events. One entry chronicled a trip by

Pope Francis, only she filled in the details of his conversations and interactions with people from the various stops as she imagined them to be. Of course, entries with this intermingling of real life and fiction were always noted at the bottom with her signature sign off: *Life according to me.*

Becoming a good writer had always been an ambition of Kate's, and she had only sought out jobs that somehow incorporated writing. After many interviews that yielded nothing but a notice that she had not been selected for the position, she finally landed an interview with Jed Ewing. Jed was the CEO of a medium—rate celebrity magazine called *What Pops.* Before the interview began, Kate had taken about twenty seconds to adjust her dress, hang her purse, and otherwise shuffle things around, always keeping her eyes down, until her potential boss had been given enough time to take her in and check over her appearance. She had read somewhere that this was a courtesy that often benefited the interviewee by allowing the interviewer to assess the person without making it awkward. The visual evaluation was always an useful tool in determining if the candidate presented themselves in a way that was appealing to the employer for the particular position being offered. It had less to do with a person's attractiveness and more to do with how they carried themselves and whether or not they paid attention to details.

Jed took full advantage of that time to notice that her black-and-tan heels were not scuffed; her light-brown hair was nicely highlighted and pulled into a classy ponytail with a lock of hair wrapped around the band that bound it all together. Her tailored black jacket and pencil skirt were fitted just enough to reveal a shapely body but were also modest and current. She wore a pale-green silk tank top underneath the jacket that had a ruffled V-neck; it was flirty, but still professional—exactly the look he wanted in a female reporter who would be representing the magazine he helped birth and who would be trying to glean interesting bits of information from famous people. She wore razor-thin gold hoop earrings and a long gold necklace that had a small sphere hanging just to the center of the two breast pockets on her jacket. Jed had a thing for long nails, and hers were French pink and nicely squared at a length not too long, but long enough to tap her leather-bound notepad when she was thinking of a response to his more difficult questions.

The interview had gone well, and she thought back to it today as she pulled into the underground parking garage at her office in Los Angeles. Jed had asked her if her necklace was a locket and if so, could he see what it was inside. His request surprised her at the time, but now that she knew him better, it was obvious that he was looking for another clue. As the years had passed and their professional relationship developed into a genuine friendship, he let her know of his obsession with finding clues that allowed him to discover things about people that they weren't necessarily aware of. In the case of her necklace, there was no picture inside it like he had expected, but a tiny colorful bead that she had to take care not to lose as she opened the locket. The bead had once been part of a necklace she had bought in Venice on one of her trips to Italy. She explained that the glass beads had been beautiful to her by themselves, but the necklace as a whole was not really her style. She wore the necklace once to justify the money spent on it, but after years of sitting neglected in a box, she decided to break it and keep the loose beads in a velvet baggie—all but one of them. This one single bead she placed inside the golden sphere to remind her of that trip. The rest of the beads would be given away to individuals who taught her something new or enriched her life in some way. She carried the velvet baggie around in her purse, and thus far, only one had been given away. She had left it on the desk of a college professor, accompanied by a note that read simply, "Thank you for unwittingly strengthening my faith in God. This bead has traveled to you from Venice and hopefully will serve as a reminder that when you give an honest challenge to your students, they will meet it."

Upon hearing this, Jed's takeaway had told him that she is willing to sacrifice a whole for a better part, that you don't always get what you expect from her, and that she stands ready to be taught and challenged. It was a good clue, and he offered her the job. At the end of the interview when it was her turn to ask questions, she asked only one: "What book are you reading right now?" He actually hadn't been reading a book at the moment but thought it might give her a bad opinion of him, so he quickly thought of his favorite novel, *The Count of Monte Cristo.*

Kate exited the parking garage via the stairs rather than the elevator. She liked to get her heart pumping a little before she sat at a desk most of the day making phone calls and answering e-mails. She abstained from drinking coffee but found her way to the Starbucks in the lobby sometimes twice a day for her ritual chocolate chai. It was warm and comforting in the same way that coffee used to be for her before she gave it up. But more than that, it was a habit—a habit which facilitated short chats with the barista who worked there and always seemed to make Kate laugh. Her name was Mozzella Outlaw. She was from the South somewhere, and her manner of speaking was sometimes hard to follow. She alternated between mumbling and loud overemphasized speech, and she used phrases that didn't always make sense to Kate, who grew up in Arizona. A quirky habit of hers was referring to herself in the third person; she did this mostly because she loved to say her own name—"Mozzella ain't playin' today ya'll, I'm on fiyah!" Emphasizing the two *z's* so it sounded more like Mozzzzella. She was also quick to point out the spelling to anyone who might not know there were two *z's* and two *l's.

"How are ya today, Mo?" Kate asked, digging for the usual lecture on not shortening her name.

Without fail, she snapped, "Don't you *dare* take a hatchet to the beautiful name my blessed momma give me! Back up a few steps Miss Kate, start ova, an' say it right... Mo-zzel-la!" As she sounded out her name, she waved her arms as if she were conducting the symphony and then punctuated it with a hearty laugh. Her full-bellied laugh always drew a giggle from Kate, who secretly wished she could sound the same when she laughed. It had a way of making the world seem right. It was the kind of laugh you wanted at your Thanksgiving table.

Kate backed up a few paces and then stepped forward with an exaggerated smile on her face. "Good morning, Mozzella! Can I have my usual?"

"Already on it. Pump o'chocolate in the cup, 'bout to be drown in spicy milk."

"Thank you. And how is your blessed momma?"

At this, she got a little hop in her step and said, "Oh, you know she hoppin' and poppin' and givin em hell! Love that woman!"

When Kate entered her office suite, she brushed past the receptionist with a quick nod of greeting. The two of them hadn't liked each other from the start, and their interactions continued to cool after Kate stepped into an uncomfortable little office tryst last year. She had stayed late one evening to finish up a piece she was writing on a former child star turned home-school mother of six. When she got to her car in the underground garage, she noticed something going on in the black Suburban parked two spaces away. Initially, she thought the occupants were fighting inside after an elbow bumped the window with a loud thud, and she heard some rough language muffled through the closed door. It's *none of my business,* she thought and started digging for her keys. Her purse was always full of random things she might need, and therefore it was always impossible to find her keys. That night, it had taken her a good thirty seconds to locate them, and in the meantime, the window of the Suburban slid down, and Sean, a coworker of hers, popped his head out sweaty and disheveled looking. Their eyes caught each other's, and immediately, he shot, "What are you looking at?" Upon his outburst, the redheaded receptionist, Jill, leaned across his lap to see who he was talking to.

"I'm looking for my keys, you jerk!" Kate spat and turned her back on them. She hadn't appreciated his accusing tone. She heard Jill tell Sean to roll up the window and get out of there, but he sat there with his gaze fixed on Kate.

"Are you going to run and tell my wife about this?" Sean had asked.

She ignored him. She had met his wife before and thought she was a nice lady. Her shock at catching him with Jill in what was obvious to her now, a front-seat hookup, kept her from knowing how to respond. It disgusted her. She wanted to say,

Yes, I'm telling her, and I hope she leaves you! But instead, she jumped in her white Touareg and drove away. On her way home that night and over the next few days, she tortured herself over whether she should expose Sean's wife to the truth. She'd gone back and forth, trying to put herself in that same situation and wondering if she had a husband who was cheating, would she want to know? Of course, she would, but would she want to hear it from his coworker? If it came in the form of an anonymous note, would she believe it? She'd had no idea what sort of marriage they had to begin with, but clearly, he was worried that it would get back to his wife, so the possibility of them being swingers was out of the question. She'd resolved to file it away for the time being and not get involved in someone else's relationship. For a fleeting second, she toyed with the idea of blackmailing him for something, but he had nothing to offer her. And she wasn't that kind of person anyway. Merely embellishing the truth ate at her, so blackmail was definitely out of the question.

Women have their ways, and Sean's wife had learned of his affair without Kate's help. One day, Sean quit without giving notice and never stepped foot in the office again. His departure was a source of bitterness for Jill, and she always suspected Kate of having a hand in it. Jed would later inform Kate that Sean's wife had called him and painted a vivid word picture of a man who could not be trusted. Sean was privately told to keep his personal affairs far away from the office, and apparently, he was so humiliated over the whole thing that he decided to quit rather than try to clean up his increasingly sleazy reputation.

Just as Kate entered her office and powered up her computer, Jill appeared at the door. She looked just as annoyed as Kate was to have to speak to each other.

"Jed wanted to see you as soon as you got in. He said it was urgent, and that you should put everything else on hold for today." Her voice was flat, and she had an air of smugness about her.

Kate didn't respond verbally; she cocked her head to the side in a *That's interesting* sort of way, remained standing, and waited for Jill to turn and leave before she picked up the phone and dialed Jed's office. There was no answer. Within seconds, her boss poked his head in her office and said, "Hiya! Did you get my message?"

"I did, just now. Tried calling you, but you're clearly not in your office. My interest is piqued. What's up?" They stood facing each other as Jed mentally sorted out how he was going to begin. He squinted at her while he rubbed his chin and then broke out into a smile.

"Tell me, who would you least expect to be booked for an interview today—with you?"

Her eyebrows rose, and she put her hands to her hips. "The only interview I have scheduled today is not really an interview but more of an introduction over the phone. That's it."

"What time is that one? Is it anyone important? Anyone I care about?"

"I'll tell you after you tell me who I'm supposedly interviewing today."

"Okay"—he couldn't hold it back anymore—"his manager actually sought us out for an interview after that piece you wrote on Joss Fenton. Apparently, he didn't like something she said and wanted to correct the record. He's going to be at the Felix today at 12:30 p.m. He said you can have an hour. An *hour*, Kate! You should be able to get some good stuff in that amount of time. And he has been off the scene for a while now, so people are going to eat it up. Do you know he's never given anyone more than fifteen minutes? At least that's what his manager said. He won't allow a camera in, but he said all topics are on the table. I'm going to push for a picture though. We need a current shot of him. He's been off the radar for a year or so, and people will want to see—"

"Who is it? You haven't given me a name yet!" Kate interrupted impatiently.

"Oh! Sorry. Are you ready for this?" He paused, waiting for her exasperated answer in the affirmative. "Lahash."

There was a long pause. The slightest shiver made its way down Kate's spine and "Wow!" was all she could manage to say. Lahash was the stage name for the lead singer of a death metal band with the same name. Death metal was the closest description available for the sound of this group. If hell itself had the face of a man and music that represented the darkness and depravity that must define such a place, it would be Lahash. It was a genre unto itself and unbelievably had a fairly large following; at least it did during the height of its success a few years ago.

She was not thrilled at this assignment and especially not with such short notice. After a failed attempt to get out of it, she shut herself in her office to prepare for the inevitable. Jed had not understood her reticence to meet face-to-face with this man. "Come on, he's just a rocker who puts on a dark show for his groupies. It's all a facade—the makeup, the demon stuff. He likes to push the envelope. You'll do fine," Jed had said. It didn't do much to assuage the anxiety welling up in Kate. Normally, she was good under pressure, and she couldn't understand why this interview was so distasteful to her. His persona gave her the creeps; she knew that when a person revels in darkness, self-regarding themselves as lord of all that debases humanity, it cannot be just skin deep. When Lahash first hit the scene, her morbid curiosity had gotten the better of her, and she had researched them—particularly the front man. He appeared mostly in gothic rags at first, but then *Rolling Stone* caught a hold of him, and he seemed to be everywhere after that. His fan club called themselves Hashers and adopted similar aspects of his look.

Kate had read somewhere that Lahash was a demon name meaning, "fallen angel who delights in thwarting divine will." His real name was Lance Ashton. Some people simply assumed that he combined letters from his first and last name to devise the stage name, but that was merely a bonus. In one account, he had described a dream of his wherein a demon had entered his mother's womb and whispered stories to him during the last three months of his gestation, and then ordered his mother to name him after his storyteller—Lahash. The story went on to say that his mother had misunderstood the demon during the throes of labor, mistakenly naming him Lance instead. Fans of the singer had tried in vain to track down his mother to inquire about his naming, but she had apparently gone into hiding. Nobody had ever interviewed his parents nor discovered the whereabouts of his only sister. Rumor told of a brother that had died at an early age, but even that was questionable. Due to the lack of family corroboration, most everything the public knew of this man's life prior to finding fame came from Lahash himself.

The band was made up of Lahash and his three myrmidons. He was the mastermind of the group; they were the wanton sidekicks. While fanatics devoured every twisted story, many people found

13

them repulsive. When the band hit their third platinum single in a row, the media world went crazy digging up sordid details of their lives. There were tales of hotel orgies clad in religious garb, satanic rituals involving animals, grotesque parties where all forms of debauchery were on display, and drug-induced trances while on stage that would be shattered only by otherworldly chants from Lahash accompanied electric guitar riffs and incessant drumbeats. This portrait of the man had been drawn for Kate through still shots and words on paper; meeting him in the flesh would bring all of that to life. Some of the stories haunted her thoughts at night when she couldn't sleep and her imagination wandered. They were images she wished had never taken form in her mind. It was a reality of this world that she wanted kept at a safe distance from her own world. Even though she had interviewed many a licentious entertainer, this one was different—he was darker.

What Pops magazine wasn't necessarily known for in-depth exposés. It was geared more toward Hollywood gossip blurbs and celebrity sightings. When Kate and her colleagues were granted an interview, it was usually a pop star on the decline looking for a little attention. They bored her. It was always a different version of the same story. At first it had been exciting to meet famous people, but gradually the luster wore off and she realized most of them were no more interesting than some other random person she might meet under different circumstances. There was one exception to that, and it was Joss Fenton.

To the general public, Joss Fenton was mostly unknown, but in the Hollywood bubble, she was an anomaly of sorts, sought after by everyone. Quiet and religious, she was the least likely to be on any A-lister's speed dial if you didn't know her talents. She was a fashion stylist and image consultant to some of the most famous celebrities. Her client list was incredible, and she had the unique ability to tailor a look that was perfect for anyone in any given situation. Name any fashion magazine, awards show, red carpet extravaganza, or media event and Joss Fenton's fingerprints were all over it. She specialized in red carpet, editorial, commercial, and advertising styling, in addition to image consulting for both men and women. But it wasn't her résumé that had interested Kate, necessarily. It was her persona overall; there seemed to be no one else like her in the entertainment industry. Kate met her only once for a quick thirty-minute sit-down for an article she was doing research for. She had wanted to shine some light on all the people whose livelihoods were supported by famous people and in addition to that, explain how they contribute to the success of the celebrities they work for. There were legions of people who fit into this category, and she thought they deserved a little credit for helping to propel the careers of others in the spotlight. When Kate had called her LA office six months prior to request an interview, Joss, whose full name was Josslyn but preferred to go by Joss, had called her back promptly and did it personally, not through her assistant. She had been extremely busy at the time with several Emmy nominees but had graciously invited Kate to meet her for lunch in between appointments.

Now that Kate was about to conduct an interview, which had come about solely because of something Joss had said to her at that lunch, she was compelled to go back and read the transcript to jar her memory of something said that may have related to Lahash. In her desk drawer, she kept a copy of every word she had ever written for *What Pops*, even the stuff that was never printed. She located the transcript and began to read:

August 12, 2014
Interview, Joss Fenton
Location, Truxton's Bistro
Duration, 37 min

KATE. Thank you for meeting with me, I know things are busy right now for you.

JOSS. No problem, I'm happy to do it. And now I have a lunch date (laugh).

KATE. Yes, this is great—I'm usually a solo eater myself, company is nice, particularly when I get to pick the brain of, someone like you. Let's just get to it, shall we?

JOSS. Of course! Try to ignore my chewing...I'm Starving!

KATE. Well, as I told you over the phone, I'd just like to learn a little bit about you, how you got your start and so forth. Did you always, want to be a style consultant?

JOSS. Umm...no, well, I've always been into fashion, but no, I never imagined in my wildest dreams I'd be doing this. I grew up in northern Virginia and was your typical DC suburbanite. I was nerdy the teenager who followed political debates, like to people-watch down on the National Mall, and spent a lot of time in the museums. My parent actually encouraged me to get a degree in poli-sci and see if I could wiggle my way into the political world by doing volunteer campaign work and stuff like that.

KATE. Did you ever do any of that?

JOSS. Once I canvassed a neighborhood for a local politician, but I didn't get very far. I stopped at this one house and started giving the guy my spiel about candidate, so-and-so, and he literally trapped me there debating the various policies and ideologies. I can't say I didn't enjoy the verbal jousting a little, but wow, that was an eye-opener for me! I was fairly young, and here I was, arguing the tax code with a complete stranger—an angry old man at that! (Laughing). No, that didn't last long. I told Mom and Dad they'd have to get the inside scoop from someone else, that I was going to do something artistic instead. I always had a flare for fashion forward avant-garde looks, even when I couldn't afford it.

KATE. Were your parents supportive? What do your siblings think of your career? If you have any, that is.

JOSS. I'm an only child. My parents were skeptical up until I got my first client. They're just happy I can pay my own bills and that it's not my face all over the magazines. Well, for this, it's okay. What I mean is, they're happy I'm not a celebrity type. They are both deeply religious and feel like that lifestyle is prone to all things evil (sarcastic laugh).

KATE. Well, that's a conversation for another day. Are you religious?

JOSS. Yes, I'm a Christian. I wandered for a while in my twenties, but some things are so ingrained in you, so undeniable that you just can't ignore it. The word *religion* seems to make people uncomfortable in this town, but if you actually break down the meaning, it's nothing more than a vehicle to the Divine. In Latin, the word *ligare* means "to tie" or "to bind." So for me, religion is what we do to tie or bind us back to God. I don't understand those people who say they believe in God but hate religion. Atheists make more sense than that, although I'd argue that they've simply replaced their faith in God with faith in man or themselves, which also doesn't make sense to me. Sorry, I could talk about this all day if you don't stop me. Do you want to hear about my first foray into the fashion world? I'm lucky I've survived in this industry long enough to find success!

Skimming through the rest of the interview, Kate could see nothing that even remotely related to Lahash. She racked her brain trying to read into her statements, and all she could come up with was that maybe he was an atheist and took issue with her opinion that they put their faith in men rather than a supreme being, something arguably more dangerous. *No, that couldn't be it,* she thought. *I seriously doubt he would ask for an interview to defend his lack of religious belief. That's almost laughable.*

She remembered the conversation with Joss being pleasant, but it took a few turns that she hadn't expected. Joss had an easy way about her. Although, you could tell she was a cerebral person and lived in her head quite a bit. There were times in the conversation where she would pause, and her eyes would be looking around as if they were taking in the visual of her memory. Her charm was that she actually listened, and she responded feeling the need to give neither flowery responses nor apologetic explanations. She was beautiful, but not in a glamorous way; her face was naturally pretty and

19

the little makeup she wore only accentuated that. Her hair was strawberry blonde and was pinned up in a messy bun on top of her head with strands hanging around her face just so. It looked casually wind-blown and professionally done at the same time. Her light blue eyes had only the slightest creases at the corners, which made her look mature, but that was the only sign of aging that could be discerned. Otherwise she looked youthful; it was hard to place her age. She was of average height and on the thin side. The day Kate met her for lunch, she had been wearing dusty purple skinny jeans over which tall leather boots hugged the bottom half of her legs. The boots were tan colored and comfortably worn in. The pointy toe and two-inch heel had a Western feel but probably had come from some upscale boutique. Her long-sleeved shirt had a brown, purple, and ivory floral print that buttoned in front and hung loosely down to the top of her thighs. There were several strands of brown wooden beads wrapped carelessly around her neck. Kate always noticed jewelry and found hers to be unpretentious. It was refreshing.

The clock had made another revolution, and she had only two and a half hours to prepare for the interview. The Felix was across town, and if traffic wasn't too thick, it would still take her about thirty minutes to get there. She didn't want to begin on an empty stomach because it would make her feel sick. She decided to give herself one hour of prep time, writing down questions, searching online, and making phone calls, and then she would head downstairs to the lobby for a drink and a sandwich. There, she would run it all through her mind and mentally gear up for what was sure to be an uncomfortable hour. She would get there early and have everything set up the way she always did. Plan in place.

After a laborious mental exercise, she had written down ten questions to ask. Then based on his responses, she would ask follow-ups. Each question was then put to the Google test to see if she could find the answers herself—at least the ones that didn't require being inside of his head to discover. Her first search entry was his name together with Joss Fenton. Their paths hadn't seemed to cross, other than she had styled people at the same music event he had performed at. Then it hit her. She picked up the phone and dialed Joss's office.

"Good morning. Fenton Consulting, can I help you?" the receptionist answered.

"Hi, yes, I'd like to speak with Ms. Fenton. Is she in?"

"No, I'm sorry. She's busy till this afternoon. I can take your name and number if you'd like a call back."

"Could you please ask her to call Kate Owens? I'm with *What Pops* magazine, and my number is...on second thought, can I just ask you a question?"

"Of course."

"Has she ever done work for or with Lahash?"

"You mean the band? No, not to my knowledge. If she had, they'd be better dressed." She gave a little snort at her remark.

"Heh, you're right. Okay, if she can't call me in the next hour don' t worry about it. Thanks."

Kate hung up before she remembered to leave her number. Oh well, it probably wouldn't help her much anyway. She'd just have to ask Lahash.

When she had prepped herself as well as she could, she decided to run it by Jed to see if he had anything to add. She knocked on his office door and waited. After a few second's, she put her ear to the door to see if he was on the phone or otherwise engaged. Just as she did so, Jill passed by the foyer to his office. She stopped short and leaned back to see what Kate was doing. Loudly she said, "Mr. Ewing's not in his office. Do you need something?" Startled, Kate shot her an irritated look and asked where he was. She took a mental note that Jill had referred to him as "Jed" when she was on his errand but as "Mr. Ewing" when she was being nosy. Jill answered that he was just stepping out for a bit, but she didn't know where he was going.

"If you don't know where he is, then why bother asking me if I need something?" Kate asked.

Jill looked taken aback, exhaled sharply, and said, "Because maybe it was something I could have helped you with."

Kate stepped toward her and tried to keep her voice even. "Well, if that were the case, I would have gone to your desk, not Mr. Ewing's office. Hmm?" She stressed his name as she said it. Kate was not prone to cattiness. She typically got along with other women. But this woman just couldn't help but get under her skin.

Heading down to the lobby, Kate hoped to find Mozzella still working. She could use a little lighthearted banter before she left on her assignment. Disappointingly, a tall, skinny redheaded man had taken over at the counter. He was nice enough, but he couldn't improve your mood the way Mozzella could. She had never learned his name, although he had worked there almost a year. Today, his long hair was braided on the sides, and he wore a beard; it was red too, naturally.

"Hi, can I have a grande, skinny, hold the water, one pump mocha chai, please?" It always irritated her to have to spell it out—not because she expected them to remember but because it made her sound picky or high maintenance, which she was not. *Or am I?* she thought. *Only when it comes to my drink. We're all allowed one thing to be picky about.*

He repeated it word for word, paused, and then smiled.

"What?"

"That's a special drink," he added with a wink.

"Aren't they all?" she said sarcastically.

"Touché! This one will be the best you've ever had. It might even cheer you up a notch."

"I'm not having a cheery day. You'll have to give it a stir if it's going to be the best. Where's Mo?"

"Mozzella is on break. You really shouldn't call her Mo. Even I'm offended now. Why are you having a bad day?"

She debated whether she should answer that seriously. "I'm about to interview Lahash."

"What! Are you serious? That band is sick! I was practically a Hasher my senior year. Can I tag along?"

Kate laughed. Before she could give another sarcastic response, she heard Jed call her name. She turned around surprised and relieved.

"Hiya! I thought I might find you here. Jill said you left for the interview, but I thought it seemed too early. Are you all set?"

"As much as I can be, I guess. Can I run a few things by you?"

He checked his watch, hesitated a moment, and then said that he didn't have time. He was meeting his wife and her boss for lunch and didn't want to be late. He added, "I will leave you with some sound advice, however. Don't go into it with an agenda. Your personal feelings, no matter what they are, should not be the driver of the interview. You've got time to let him bloviate a little, and I guarantee he'll give you something to chew on. They know when you're pushing them in a certain direction, and this guy seems intelligent despite his looks. I can't wait to hear all about it. And look for clues! You know me. I rely on the things unsaid as much as I do things said. Oh yeah, meet at the front desk and the maître d' will show you where to set up. Call me later." He was already making his way to the elevator as he finished.

Well, that was a lot of help," she muttered to herself. She took her cup and headed to a small table tucked away behind the product stands where she hoped no one would bother her. It was to no avail because seconds later, the barista stepped over and asked if he could interrupt her for a minute. *Mr. Red Braids again.* She nodded her head in consent only because her drink was made perfectly, to her delight.

"I've always wanted to know something about Lahash." He waited for a prompt, but she said nothing. "Well, I was just wondering if you could ask him about one of his tattoos. He has a little brain with a question mark on it. All the other ones make sense—the red dragon, the fire, the sculls, and all that—but the brain tat has me mystified. Could you ask him what it represents? What's the meaning of it? I ask because...well, look."

He rotated his left arm to the back and pointed out his own tattoo of a brain, only his had a dark cloud behind it. He explained that he got the tattoo because his father was mentally ill, and although the sickness had never been accurately diagnosed, his father's erratic and bizarre behavior had been like a storm cloud partially blocking the sunshine in his life. For some reason, his story pricked at Kate's heart, and she agreed to ask the question. She hoped it would have some meaning behind it; if not for the mere fact that it was permanently emblazoned on his skin but to give this guy a satisfactory answer.

"What is your name anyway?" she asked.

"Taylor, but feel free to call me Leif. All my friends do."

"Why Leif?"

"One, because I like it better, and two, because Leif Erikson had red hair. You know, the crazy Viking son of Erik the Red? He discovered North America, Newfoundland to be exact, five hundred years before Columbus came, or so I'm told. He deserves more credit, if you ask me."

"I'm Kate. You can call me Kate. Nice to meet you, Leif."

2

*T*he Felix was a new hotel that had been built in the footprint of an old office building that had once stood there. Its style was modern, although it had a classic edge. Amidst the strait lines and simple design of everything from the architecture to the furniture, was mingled in black-and-white portraits of vintage LA. There were pictures of Sunset Boulevard *circa* 1950 and iconic buildings from surrounding areas. Large glass vases of fresh white flowers dotted the lobby, their scent delightfully impeding the overwhelming smell of new carpets and paint, which hadn't yet receded after its scant two weeks of business. It was Kate's first look at the inside of the building, although she had watched its outside take form throughout the construction process. Neither the exterior nor the interior impressed her much. But it was new and therefore felt clean. There was nothing that she disliked more than to step into a hotel that seemed to have a layer of unseen filth coating every surface and air fresheners that tried mightily to disguise the still lingering smell of cigarette smoke from times passed when it was still legal to smoke indoors in most places.

Kate made her way to the front desk and informed the dark-suited employee she was there to interview Lahash. After checking her credentials, the maître d' escorted her down a long hallway. At the far end of the hallway, they met a small elevator that indicated it was for staff only. He gestured for her to enter and then punched in floor number 11. They smiled briefly at each other on the way up but said nothing. The hallway, which opened to them was bright with windows running the full length of the wall on the right side. On the left side, there were two unmarked doors, both of which had arched wooden doorframes that didn't seem to fit with the rest of the design scheme in the hotel. The carpet was a plush cream color, and the walls were dark beige; the only ornamentation were two oiled bronze wall sconces on either side of each door.

"Right here, ma'am." The maître d' walked just ahead of her and pulled out a key card. He inserted it into the first of the two doors.

"Is this a conference room?" she asked, slightly puzzled.

"No, ma'am. This floor has two VIP guest suites. This one is unoccupied, and it has been requested that you conduct the interview here. I'll notify Mr. Weiz that you've arrived."

His accent sounded like he was from the northeast somewhere, but she couldn't place it. She followed him into a spacious sitting room and took a look around.

"Will you need anything before I go? Water? A glass of wine?" he asked.

"No, thank you. I've brought what I need."

"When you've finished, please ring the front office and I'll be back to escort you down to the lobby. My name is Gabe."

She slipped him a tip and thanked him again. She was about to ask who Mr. Weiz was, but she assumed he must be Lahash's manager and left it at that. There was rarely an interview where the celebrity didn't have some sort of entourage with them, and if it wasn't the manager, it was some other PR person along with anyone else they needed to make themselves feel comfortable.

With fifteen minutes to go, she decided to get familiar with the space. The sitting room was at the center of the suite. It had large windows directly opposite the entrance door that were bedecked with mocha-colored drapes that hung from ceiling to floor. The walls had some sort of textured brown paneling, which was framed on the outer edges with pale-gold wall paint. A velvet couch was flanked on either side by two club chairs, and in the center was a black-and-gold metal coffee table. Behind the couch sat a wingback chair with a couch-length desk and a telephone. Off to the right side, there was a closed door with a look-through fireplace on the wall; the left side opened to a slightly smaller room with a large flat-screen TV, a minibar, and several lounge chairs. The floor was made of dark wood planks that were set in a square pattern, but it was mostly covered by a sprawling rug. The paintings on the walls were like those in the lobby—black-and-white images; only these ones were international scenes.

Checking all the doors, she found a powder room, a full bathroom that looked more like a spa, and a handsomely decorated bedroom. The look-through fireplace was shared with the bedroom. Kate thought that was an interesting setup, given that it provided a glass window of sorts from the sitting room into the bedroom. Looking from the bedroom side, you could see straight into the other room, but from the sitting room side, she discovered that the glass was tinted enough that you had to look very closely to make out the bed. The full bathroom also had an electric fireplace, but it was set about shoulder height on the wall and looked more like a curved TV screen.

Kate decided to sit in one of the club chairs and allow Lahash the option of sitting across from her in the other club chair or to her left side on the couch. She laid out her leather binder with the questions she had written, along with some notes and the voice recorder she would use to type the transcript later. She also brought along a small camera, which she kept in her pocket. When they had more time to plan, they usually brought along a photographer to take pictures if the subject was amenable to it. In this case, she hadn't had time to arrange all of that, so she brought her own camera just in case. She would get a feel for his mood before requesting a photo. He may be offended that she didn't bring a professional, or he may just provide his own. Either way, she knew Jed wanted a current shot, and this was the best she could do. She did a quick check on the voice recorder and then set two water bottles out on the coffee table.

After sitting a few minutes, she got up and began to pace. She couldn't decide if she wanted to be standing or sitting when he arrived. For some reason, she started to feel self-conscious and started fidgeting with her hair and clothes. Her tan slacks were feeling too tight around the waist, and she wished she had pulled her hair back away from her face. Today, she had left it to its natural wave instead of employing the flat iron. She checked her watch twice and started to feel a little anxious that it was now five passed the hour. Recalling a TED Talk she had listened to once, she decided to try a little exercise that was meant to give you a boost of confidence before doing something that made you nervous. The speaker had said that if you stood in front of a mirror for two minutes in a Superman stance, or in other words, with your chest out and your arms and legs apart, that it would make you feel a sense of power. A side benefit was that you would also feel slightly ridiculous and laugh at yourself, which would decrease stress and help you to relax. Kate stepped in front of the mirror on the wall and did her best power stance. Her legs were about shoulder width apart, and she placed her hands on her hips. She puffed out her chest and lifted her chin and tried to hold the position for a minute. They were right; she felt ridiculous and smiled at herself.

She jumped and spun around just then as the door latch clicked. A man in a gray suit entered and smiled in her direction. *Did he see me jump?* She wondered. Kate smiled back and walked over to make introductions.

Oliver Weiz was a short man who sported a salt-and-pepper buzz cut and perfect white teeth. His skin was tanned, and he had a strong grip of a handshake. He wore several chunky silver rings but otherwise looked like a straight-talking businessman. He explained to Kate that he had been with Lahash since the beginning and found this situation a little strange. Lahash had never asked anyone to interview him. In fact, he usually loathed doing them. In the early days, Oliver had nearly forced him to make interviews so that his name recognition would grow.

"Well, I hope he doesn't regret this when all is said and done. Is he ready?" she asked.

"Yes, he'll be in shortly. I just wanted to reiterate his desire for no video or pictures."

Kate looked disappointed. She indicated that there was no cameraman with her but asked if they had a current photo they would let her have to publish with the interview. He promised to send something over and then excused himself.

She removed the camera from her pocket and dropped it into her purse. *Well, that's that.*

Just as she sat back down, the door opened again, and her reason for coming entered the room. The whole mood of the room changed when Lahash crossed the threshold. Her mind jumped momentarily to a book series she'd read years ago, and she imagined that he was a life-sucking ghost entering the room, causing the temperature to drop and happy thoughts to flee from her being. She stood and walked over to shake his hand, unable to take her eyes off him. He was taller than he looked on TV. Kate was five feet ten, and he had to be at least six inches taller than she was. His face was pale white except for the purplish black lipstick and the dark eyeliner around his eyes. It was impossible to decipher the real color of his eyes because he wore black contacts that covered the entirety of his iris, with no distinction of a pupil. His hair was jet-black and pulled back into a loose ponytail at the nape of his neck; it was tousled and messy and hung just past his shoulder blades. His attire looked as though it had come from the mid-1800s, minus the black leather pants. He wore a white button front shirt that was undone down to his chest, a red silk vest, and a black tailcoat jacket that draped in the back down to his knees with the front waist length. His black leather pants were tucked neatly into his squared-toed boots. The most interesting item was the black top hat that sat just off center of his head. He looked like a character from a vampire movie, except he had none of the seductive charm. Rather, he seemed withdrawn and out of his element.

Kate extended her hand and introduced herself. He seemed reluctant to shake it but did it anyway, albeit so lightly that it was more like brushing fingertips. His behavior was odd; she expected more confidence maybe. This gesture brought his long fingernails to her attention, and she involuntarily recoiled. She imagined all the cocaine that must have been scooped and snorted with the help of those nails or the flesh that may have been scratched and torn with them. She decided against closing the interview with the customary handshake. But that was a full hour away. At this moment, it seemed like an eternity to her.

"I thought I'd sit here," Kate said, gesturing toward the chair with her stuff near it. "Please sit wherever you like, and we'll get started."

"I think I'd like to sit there," he said in a deep voice. It was the chair Kate had selected to sit in.

"Oh! Okay, sure, no problem. I'll just move my stuff to the other side." Just as she started gathering up her notes, he put his hand on her arm and laughed briefly.

"Don't ever do that," he said.

"What?" she asked confused.

"Don't give up your seat so easily. I'm not the president!" he sneered and then punctuated it with an ugly expletive.

"Okay." She laughed awkwardly and waited until he sat in the club chair opposite her before she sat down.

This little stunt of his threw her off slightly, making her unsure of how to begin. He began for her.

"Does my appearance offend you?" he asked.

"No but the f-word does," she said sheepishly.

A look of unveiled surprise flashed across his face, and he laughed out loud. It was a guttural laugh that barely showed in his eyes. He looked amused and said, "Well, that's one of my favorite adjectives. What ever shall I replace it with?"

His tone was mocking. And she vacillated between actually suggesting an alternative word and ignoring it altogether. She decided it was rhetorical and left his question hanging in the air. She showed him her voice recorder, switched it on, and explained that she would be recording from here on out. He gave one nod of assent. Then she placed it on the coffee table and began her questioning.

"Since you brought up your appearance, why did you choose that look? Are you trying to offend people?" She sat poised with her pen in hand. Even though she relied on the voice recorder to catch what was said, she still liked to take notes on what was not said, such as body language or other gestures that might be good to remember later.

"No. I'm just being what I am. If that offends people, I don't care. I actually find it amusing."

"But why the black eyes and the eighteen-century attire? Is there a reason why you choose to present yourself in that fashion? It comes across as dark...even satanic."

"The outside is a reflection of the inside. It matches my music. I'm consistent—which is to say, I'm a rarity. Most people aren't genuine. They host demons on the inside, but outwardly, they look like the sweet mom in an apron. Or it's the opposite—

those are the really messed up ones. They're the guys who are decent but build this bad guy facade. And for what? Just be who you are. If you're 'satanic,' embrace it." At this, he took off his hat and tossed it on the couch then laid back in the chair with his arms open wide, as if to say, *Look at me. I've embraced it totally.*

Deciding to try a different tack, she asked, "I was told you asked for this interview to set the record straight on something Joss Fenton said. Do you want to tell me what that is?"

He sat looking at her for a moment. She waited expectantly. Then he got up and moved over to the couch, sitting on the end closest to her, close enough that their knees might touch. He leaned forward and looked directly into her eyes. It was unnerving to look into those black eyes with only the slightest white showing around the corners. His face looked more like a mask to her, and he smelled strongly of cigarette smoke.

Then he simply stated, "I'm still alive." His gaze remained directed at her, but he leaned back against the couch and said nothing else. Kate was confused.

"What? I'm sorry, what does that mean?"

"I breathe. I walk. I exist."

Still clearly confused, she asked, "And what does that have to do with Joss Fenton?"

"Not a bloody thing, apparently. Did you catch that courtesy I just offered you?" he said smiling.

"Huh?"

"Bloody! I said the word *bloody*. New adjective, remember?"

"Oh, yeah, thanks. Wait—why did you feel the need to state that you're still alive?"

He inhaled and exhaled slowly. "Somebody will figure that out someday. New topic? Ask me anything." He slowly removed his jacket. His movements communicated that he had said what he came to say, and now he would endure the rest of the time as a favor to her.

Her eyes moved in a circle as if they were still searching for an answer. Before she could think of what to say next, he asked her a question instead. "Do you believe in God?"

"Yes..." Her head tilted to the side as if to ask why he wanted to know.

"I don't," he said simply. " Evil and goodness are subjective. People call my music satanic, but there's freedom in aggression and just doing whatever you want. I feel no societal constraints to behave a certain prescribed way. There is beauty in that. I've done things that would make others cringe, but I can do it without reservation, without the chains of guilt." Then he crossed his legs and smiled, implying that the ball was in her court now to speak.

"Are all those things true then? The things they write about you in magazines? The drugs, the animal rituals, the orgies, all that? Or is it sensational and exaggerated?"

"Just assume it's all true."

His comment and the look on his face made her skin crawl. She really didn't want to hear the details but felt compelled to ask, "Is there any line you wouldn't cross? Any act that's too abhorrent, even for you?"

"I don't give myself any barriers. But I don't want to wind up locked in a cage either, so I guess mass murder is out of the question." He smirked. "I would never have kids. That's where I draw the line."

Thank goodness for that! she thought. "Well, I guess that makes sense. But I'm curious as to why not?"

"The closest I ever want to get to a kid is my girlfriend's unfertilized eggs."

"So I guess a normal life is out of the question for you. I mean, you've done everything else, pushed every boundary. I guess if you really wanted to shock people, you'd have to do the normal thing—

get married, have kids, wear a suit and tie, and live in the suburbs."

"Well, there's a paradigm shift for you! Yeah, I guess if I truly wanted to live an alternative lifestyle these days, I'd have to put the monkey suit on and have a family." He laughed at the thought.

"So why not try it?"

There was a long pause while he waited for her to crack a smile or show that she was being sarcastic and then blurted out, "What? Are you serious?" He looked incredulous.

She seemed deep in thought for a second, and her eyes wandered away from him. She wondered if it were possible for a man like Lahash to do an about face in life and be able to pull it off. There were too many examples of people who did the opposite. There were so many people who were raised in a good family, with morals and values, which later in life turned away from that and lived a depraved life. Sometimes it was because of a series of bad choices, sometimes it was the harsh reality of life that threw them off the path, and sometimes they just chose to turn from the good and embrace the bad. Hollywood was an endless parade of bubbly, bright-eyed child stars who later wound up in some dingy drug den. Or they were the girl next door from small-town America who got a big break with a dose of fame, and the next thing you know, she has renounced her childhood religion and she's posing nude in *Playboy*

41

or acting out some erotic lesbian scene in a movie. Some of them were thrust into an adult world and didn't know any better. Others were led by a velvet chord around their neck into a life of debauchery, thinking that that was how they could get more money or fame. She wondered which case he fell into.

It wasn't just in Hollywood either. The story was a common one. Rarely did she hear of people who did the reverse, turning from a life of sin and misdeeds to a life of service to others, or what have you. Surely those stories existed, but not in the public arena. In the media, it was the fallen angels who were celebrated as being "liberated," "edgy," and "interesting." Those who deliberately chose a life of service, of believing in God, of family, and of goodness were derided in the media as simpleminded—no, close minded—idiots, not worthy of paying any attention to. It was an illness of the popular culture, and in this moment, she wished for someone who would flip it on its head, reverse the same old sad story and give up everything to gain something better. Looking him over again, she decided to see if she could direct their conversation around to it. She wanted to see if there was any inkling of a chance. Call it a social experiment.

"What was your childhood like?"

He made a noise with his throat and looked up at the ceiling. "Let me guess, you want to know if I was abused or otherwise driven to the dark side, right?"

"Well, were you? I'm trying to picture you as a ten-year-old boy. What were you like then? Did you play sports? Did you have a lot of friends?"

He gave a sardonic laugh and brushed it off by saying he had a charmed childhood. She pressed further, asking about his relationship with his parents.

"My parents were psychos who should have never had children, if you want the truth. I was the way I am from as young as I can remember, so they didn't drive me to be anything I wasn't already. But they certainly did not know how to deal with me. Sports? Yeah, if you count running from your dad or dodging your mom's projectiles as a sport. At ten, I was already drawing tattoos on my arms with a permanent marker and cussing like a pro."

"I want to get back to your parents in a second, but you just reminded me of something. Do you have a tattoo of a brain and a question mark?"

His eyebrows rose, and he stood up. "You mean this?" He lifted his shirt at the waist and pushed his pants down uncomfortably low so she could see the tattoo that sat just above his pelvic bone. Against his white skin, the color of the brain looked reddish gray and the squiggly lines of brain formed a question mark. It was gruesome in its design and position.

"Uh, yes. I didn't know it was located there, but yes. What does it represent?"

"You are the first person to ask me about that—other than the guy who gave it to me. How did you know I had it?"

"One of your fans is curious."

He gave her a devious look as if to imply that she was the fan. "Oh really? Well, tell my fan that it's private. We need to be better acquainted to share that."

"I personally don't care what it means. But there is a Hasher out there who knows about it and has a pretty good reason for asking." He laughed at the mention of the word *Hasher* but gave her a look to go on. "Before he became a fan of your music, he got a similar tattoo on his arm. It's a brain with a cloud behind it. He told me it was because his dad has a mental illness, which was like a cloud overshadowing his life. He wondered if yours had significant meaning as well. I promised him I'd ask."

He seemed to be debating what to say in his mind. And then she saw it; even with those black eyes, the wall came down, and she knew he wouldn't tell her. Regardless, she waited for his excuse. None came. He just sat there blankly. So she decided to move on.

"Would you like to take a break? Do you need a drink or anything before we move on?" she asked.

"A drink! Good call. "He got up and went to the minibar. He came back with a small bottle of liquor and offered one to her. She politely declined, not only did she not drink alcohol, but she especially wouldn't drink it with this man alone in a hotel room. So he gulped down both and sat back visibly more relaxed.

She went back to her notes and the questions she had written earlier that morning. Deciding to go with her favorite question in all situations, work or otherwise, she asked, "What book are you reading now?"

Without skipping a beat, he popped off his response, "The Bible."

"Huh!" It was a statement, not a question. She was shocked at the quickness of that response and disbelieving as well. He could tell.

"You don't believe me? I read it all the time. 'An educated person knows the Bible,' the old billboard says. And every time I see it, I agree. It gives me inspiration for lyrics and enhances my stage performance. I played a show in Utah once, of all places, and right there on stage, I danced out all the rituals of animal sacrifices, sin offerings, wave offerings, all that detailed in the books of Moses. Leviticus is hard to get through, but you can really draw some crazy stuff from it. And yes, I am educated, self-educated mostly. I'm a voracious reader. I like to pick the most difficult writers and topics and just chew on them for a while until I understand them. And then I read trash novels in between to still feel normal. And you, my dear?"

"What?"

"What are you reading at the moment?"

"Oh. I'm reading..." *What book do I want to tell him? I don't really want to clue him in that I'm studying body language. Who knows where he'll take that.* Atlas Shrugged? *No, no politics.* The truth was that she wanted to shock him with a title he wouldn't expect, like he had done, but she couldn't think of anything.

He broke into her thought process. "What, it is a secret? Let me guess, you're reading some epic sadomasochistic fantasy book and you're afraid of what your colleagues will think of that? No, you don't seem the type. Maybe *Mein Kampf?*" He leaned forward and lightly touched her knee and said, "Tell me about your childhood." This last part he said with feigned concern.

The way he turned it back at her was irksome, and she retorted, "Are you doing the interview here, or am I?"

He was amused that he had gotten to her. So he continued, "Well, it's starting to feel more like a therapy session than an interview. Do you want me to lie down on the couch and dissect my relationship with my parents?"

"No, I want you to be a true 'rarity' and reverse course." *What!* her mind screamed. Her hands started to shake, but she continued with what she had verbally stepped into. He had a surprised and quizzical look on his face. "You said you were a 'rarity' because your inside matches your outside. Well, I hate to break it to you, but that's not that rare. What is hardly ever witnessed in the public arena is a man who is brave enough to give up his self-serving, indulgent life for a better one. And by that, I mean he won't sacrifice his image or career in order to seek out a life that is truly good. Some things we are inherently born with, such as eye color or personality, but most of what we become is through choices. You have *chosen* to be this"—she gestured in his direction at nothing in particular— "and you can *choose* to be different. I want to see if it's possible. You would be the perfect poster boy to see if by your will alone you can turn a demon, no offense, into an angel, as a matter of speaking. And the challenge would be if you could do it sincerely. If you did, it would be fascinating to watch how the public responds." She could almost hear Jed screaming in her ear, *Don't go into it with an agenda!* Her boldness even caught her by surprise.

"Are you...is this...what are you doing? Are you actually challenging me to become a family man who goes to church or something?" he stammered.

"Yes."

"That's f—crazy!" he shouted and then laughed uproariously. His smile even reached his eyes, and his deep voice cackled around the room. When he finally composed himself again, his purplish shade of black lipstick had pale-pink lines showing through it from his lips being stretched into a smile. He failed to notice her cringe at the use of his favorite adjective, but she let it slide given that he was laughing. She saw a glimpse there, however small. It was a glimpse of the man, not the character—of Lance, not Lahash.

Kate put her notes to the side and earnestly tried to explain her thought process to him.

"It's crazy only insofar as it's something that nobody would ever expect from you or someone like you. But let me tell you a story, a parable, if you like, since you're familiar with the Bible"

"Humor me," he interjected.

"There was a girl that was brought up in a church, raised in a good family. She grew up to serve in the military and later marry and have children. She went back to school to get her degree in architecture, and her husband supported her doing landscaping work. While studying, she came across literature that was anti-capitalist, and she was naturally skeptical of it because capitalism is the economic driver of this country. She read it for the class but mostly dismissed it as left-wing propaganda. Later, her husband lost his job and couldn't find another one that suited him. There was work to be had, although he thought himself above it and began to lie and cheat to make money rather than make an honest living. When things became really bad for them financially, they turned to the church. The church provided them a humble living, but it was not what they were used to, and pride drove them away from that support system into the faceless yet fatherly hands of government welfare. Relying on welfare checks and living with various family members, they began to be bitter about life and dispensed blame for their sorry situation on anyone but themselves. Soon, that bitterness bled into other aspects of their lives, and they gave up religion and their faith in God vanished. And predictably, they blamed the capitalist system and embraced the dogma of socialism. The seed had been planted earlier for this ideological flip-flop, and then choices and circumstances led to the total acceptance of it. Now this woman is an angry, secular, antibusiness activist. Her children will be taught the dogma that she once despised, therefore perpetuating the cycle. And because socialism has never worked and will never work in this country, she will remain angry and bitter—just what we all would expect, right? But what if one day she woke up and decided she wanted a better life? What if she took a job as a waitress and convinced her husband to be a taxi driver, anything just to be free of dependence on the government—and the capitalism that supports it. They become self-reliant, save up enough to buy a house, and then eventually move up the economic ladder until they can live comfortably, doing what they always wanted to do. She finishes her degree in architecture and becomes a great success. She starts her own firm and is able to hire others who will follow her path to prosperity. Isn't this the story we would prefer to hear? Wouldn't society be better for it? Yet it doesn't happen very often. People prefer to be left in their proverbial chains so long as they look cool in today's culture and they don't have to work hard at anything."

He waited patiently for her to finish and then stated blandly. "I'm already a rich capitalist."

"You're missing my point," she said, frustrated.

"No, I get it, but you don't get *me*. My goal in life is to please myself not to make society a better place. Screw society."

"It's not about that either, necessarily. It's about choices...never mind."

She brought it back to his childhood and what his parents had been like. He was clearly reluctant to talk about it, but she probed more about his mother's projectiles and why he would have to run away from his dad. Finally, he agreed to tell her one story. As he started relating it, he stood and sauntered around the room, pausing now and again to collect his thoughts.

"I'm a twin. Bet you didn't know that. Most people don't. You know why? Because he died in the womb. I killed him—at least according to my parents. My mom treated me like a criminal even as a toddler. She'd lock me in my room for no reason. If I cried, she would just remind me that my dead baby brother couldn't cry, so I didn't deserve any comfort. Yeah, she gave me food and I had a roof over my head, but I never felt wanted. It was as if losing that baby hardened them so much that they couldn't love me. Don't feel pity. I was a hell raiser, especially as a young teen."

"One time I ditched school and ran off to this old shed back in the woods. It was actually an abandoned house that was all grown over with weeds and vines. I went there a lot to smoke pot and be alone. But this time, I wasn't alone. It was the craziest thing—this girl showed up, wearing a long black cloak, and she had blond, blond hair, almost white. She was fifteen, or so she said, and I was thirteen at the time. I lost my virginity that day. After that, we would meet up and plan this new world together. I was the idea maker who would tell her how everything should be, and she was the witch who had power to make it all happen. We both found an escape in each other and this fantasy world. I have no idea what her story was, and she never told me her name. Anyway, we decided we needed money or some way we could buy a few things for our little meeting place. Its roof was falling in, so we'd get soaked whenever it rained.

Plus the floor boards were so rotten we fell through a few times and cut up our legs. So we lifted a few things from the Dollar Store, like plastic ponchos to stuff in the ceiling, towels, and cardboard for the floor. But it still wasn't comfortable, so we hatched a plan to remove the mattress from my bed and carry it out there one night. My dad was traveling, and my mom was busy watching TV in her bedroom, so nobody noticed as we lugged this twin-size mattress out the door and across the field into the woods.

"Well, that shack became my new home. I'd rip off food from my parents whenever I could, and I never went to school. This lasted for like a month, and my parents never even noticed. They were probably so happy to not have me around to fight with that they didn't bother asking any questions. Until the school called them and told them I'd been absent for too long. Since they were surprised by this news, the police came asking questions. After they left, my dad was furious! He came to my room to confront me about my truancy, and that's when they noticed that my mattress was gone. When I refused to tell them where it was, my dad beat me like you wouldn't believe. I called him a few choice words, and he shipped me off to live with his sister-in-law in North Carolina. She was an old hag who never had kids, so she was the perfect person to shove me off onto. She let me do what I wanted because I was too much to handle for her. I got into heavy drugs and left at the age of seventeen with a little band I had formed called Wet Mattress. I haven't talked to my parents since. And we all lived happily ever after."

"So you've had no contact with your parents since you were thirteen? That's hard to believe, "said Kate.

"Well, I heard they had started a new life in another state from my aunt. She gave me updates once in a while, and presumably she gave them updates about me. But even she had no idea where I went after I left her place." He gulped down another bottle of liquor and laid back lazily on the couch.

"So you've been on your own since you were seventeen. Interesting. Did Wet Mattress ever have any success?"

"Just enough to keep me going with music. Two of my original band members are still with me. After our drummer died, we moved to New York and regrouped. We met Ox, our drummer in Lahash, and he really helped us change our sound. He introduced us to the right people, and by age twenty, I'm in California making my first record."

"Well, that's quite a journey. But now you've found success. Are you happy with where you are now?"

"No, I'm just a 'demonic' rock star. I would be much happier if I lived in Idaho and could hold hands with my lovely wife as we strolled to church on Sunday mornings." He looked over at her to gauge what her response would be.

She returned his gaze and said simply, "I'd love to meet Lance Ashton someday."

The remainder of the interview lasted about fifteen more minutes. Lahash's mood had been considerably lighter than at the first. Of course, the alcohol could have contributed to that. But Kate knew that her challenge to him hit a chord. She knew it, not by what he said but rather by the way he would sit back now and again and rub his chin with his thumb and index finger as if considering the possibilities. Then he would make some crack at how ridiculous it was for her to suggest it, as if he were trying to convince himself that it was totally out of the question. She didn't press it. Her final question to him was to ask if she could snap a photo of him with her camera. She had promised that it would not be used if he didn't like how it came out, but that her boss gave her a direct charge to do everything in her power to get a recent picture of him. To her surprise, he consented—on one condition: He wanted a side view only.

He stood directly in front of a window that had light streaming in, so that only his silhouette would be visible. The top hat had been returned to his head and positioned at a tilt on the side facing the camera. He placed his hands on the back of the desk chair and looked down and slightly to the side, as if peering out the corner of his eye. She squared the frame at about the center of his thighs and up enough to clear his hat. Just one click, and then he broke pose. He took a look at the image on her digital screen and said, "You're a better photographer than interviewer." With that, he turned and slowly left the room. She managed to call out "Thank you for your time!" just before the door clicked shut.

3

*A*fter Kate left the Felix, she didn't bother going

back to the office. It was late afternoon, and she wanted to get a start on the drive home before traffic slowed to a halt. She had been pleased with how the interview had gone for the most part but was relieved to be done with it. When she had set out for work that morning, she had no idea she would wind up spending the afternoon with Lahash. He was interesting; she had to give him that. And despite her predisposition to dislike him, she had actually enjoyed the conversation in the end. He was unsettling to look at, and she still hated his music, but she had the feeling she would see him again.

Kate rented a small condo off North Figueroa Street near Pasadena. She decided to check her phone just as she exited Interstate 110. There were several calls and a text from Jed telling her to call him when she got a chance. In order to keep her eyes on the road, she decided to wait till she got home to do that.

Her beeline for the door was impeded by a large box in the walkway. She lived on the ground floor and shared only one wall with a neighbor. Thankfully, that neighbor was a good friend. *The box must belong to Markus*, she thought. If not, she would be seriously annoyed. She inched her way between the wall and the box while needlessly sucking in her stomach. Markus appeared from his doorway just as she passed.

"Hey there, neighbor! You're just in time. I need to move this box into my living room."

"Really? How did you get it here in the first place? I have to call my boss. Sorry, bud, next time!"

Markus persisted, "James was supposed to help me, but he's taking too long. I got it here myself, but I can't maneuver it through the doorway. Go change your clothes and make your phone call, and then come back and help a brother out!"

She gave him an annoyed look over her shoulder and started to make another excuse about having a busy day and just wanting to relax, but he offered to make her dinner before she could finish the thought.

Markus was a great cook and Kate was hungry. "Deal," she said. "Give me a minute."

Jed was anxious to hear about how the interview went. She tried to give him the condensed version with a promise to get the transcript to him by close of business tomorrow, but he wanted to hear it all. She started from the beginning and told him everything she could remember, but she glossed over the part where she had basically dared him to completely reinvent himself. He pestered her with questions about why he had asked for the interview in the first place, which she couldn't exactly answer. She tried to end the conversation by telling him she was late for a dinner date.

"Wow, you've got a date tonight?" Jed asked, genuinely interested. He had tried to set her up with several guys from his poker club, but only one had resulted in a date. It was a miserable failure, and Kate wouldn't let him forget it.

"Yes, a date. Don't sound so surprised."

"Who is he?"

She hesitated, "Um, just a guy in my neighborhood. No big deal." She was trying to sound nonchalant about it, even though there was nothing romantic to it.

"Oh, I see. It's Markus, isn't it?" She rolled her eyes. "Kate, seriously, he sounds like a nice guy, but that's not a date. You two have been friends for years now. That doesn't count."

Her boss could read her better than her parents could—which made sense because she talked to him on a daily basis, and she only talked to them a handful of times a year.

"Well, he's cooking for me, so it counts. Anyway, I'd prefer to spend time with someone I know and like rather than a complete stranger that I have to pretend to be interested in. You're lucky to be happily married and well into a comfortable life together. Stop rubbing it in that I'm not there yet. I'll see you in the morning."

Jed always waxed poetic when he talked about his family. Everyone in his circle of friends knew about how lucky he was to have Deborah in his life. Not only because he continually said it, but because she had literally rescued him from death twice. Once from a bout of depression that nearly drove him to end his life, and another time she had resuscitated him after he had stopped breathing in his sleep. Furthermore, it was she who had introduced him to Christianity, and he credits her for his eternal happiness. They had four children. The older two were married and lived nearby; one was at home finishing up high school, and the other one was currently stationed in Texas serving in the army. For Kate, who had spent many holidays with the Ewings, they were the ideal family. They vacationed together, they talked all the time about everything,

59

and they still had Sunday dinners together. They seemed to be a dying breed.

Markus had offered to help Kate with a flat tire when she first moved into the condo. She was new to the area and didn't know what she would have done without him. At the time, he had been married but had divorced about a year ago. Kate and Sheila got along fine, but she knew Sheila had been unfaithful to Markus, and so she encouraged him to sign the divorce papers when Sheila sprung them on him. He hadn't wanted to because he still loved her and thought they could work it out. Markus is the eternal optimist. He dreaded the idea of being single again, but Sheila moved out and left him with no choice but to sign the papers. Since then, Kate had become his go-to person for everything. If he needed a dog sitter, he asked Kate. If he wanted company while he washed his car, he asked Kate. If he had leftovers from dinner, he took them to Kate. And she likewise relied on him for many things. He helped her move heavy furniture, fix her computer, connect her TV, and other tasks that were easier with a man's help. But more than that, he was her sounding board when she just needed to talk and sort things out. She could count on him for good advice in most cases, and she enjoyed his company. Their relationship had remained platonic, mostly because he was still shell-shocked over the divorce, and neither of them was emotionally open to a romantic relationship. If you asked her, Kate would say she found him on the attractive side of the scale. He was average height, and his Cuban ancestry had blessed him with olive-toned skin and dark features. His hair was black and short, but he always wore a ball cap, so it was covered most of the time. He sported a salt-and-pepper goatee, and his eyes were deep brown. For his day job, he did IT work for a small online company. On his off time, he helped his sister paint and restore old furniture, which she would then sell at a markup and give him a cut of the profits.

With much effort, they managed to squeeze the box through Markus's front door.

"What is this thing?" Kate asked.

"An antique desk. You're going to love this sucker. It's got a slab of African sapele on top that's about three inches thick. I'll open it after we eat. It will be the second dessert."

"Where did you get it? It's got to weigh at least two hundred pounds!"

"I don't reveal my secrets. Let's just say I worked my magic and came out lucky. I can make a good profit on this if I find the right buyer. That is, if I don't decide to keep it myself. Although, I hate to disgrace it with my shabby place here." He motioned toward the cheap Ikea furniture in the living room. Sheila had taken all the good furniture, leaving Markus to throw together a cheap alternative. It was ironic, given that he refurbished furniture, which sold for sometimes 150 percent over what they originally paid for it.

They conversed casually while Markus banged pots and pans in the kitchen, flipping spice jars, and throwing together a savory arroz con pollo with avocado salad on the side. Kate's version of a homemade dinner was the 8:00 p.m. omelet.

While they ate, she related the day's events to him. He listened politely until she got to the end, and then he chided her for not asking for more details about Lahash's relationship with Joss Fenton. She admitted it was a failure on her part, but she honestly felt that he wouldn't tell her any more.

"He wanted to get a message to someone, and he did. It made no sense to me, but what else could I do?" Kate protested.

"You could start by not letting him get away with cryptic messages that only beg more questions. Seriously, your boss is going to take you to task over that. Speaking of Jed, what did he think of the whole 'Stop being a demonic waste of a human being and have a family instead' rigmarole?"

She shrugged her shoulders and took another bite, avoiding his questioning look. He chuckled and said, "You didn't tell him, did you? Wow, sister, you're on a roll! First you botch the most intriguing part of this whole thing, and then you challenge an iconoclast rocker to be more like Mitt Romney or something. That's classic. What in the world were you thinking?"

"I don't know. There's only so far a person can push the limits, and then it becomes expected and just blends into the background. Guys like him are always looking for ways to shock people, and honestly, there's nothing that would be more shocking than a total about face. The media would go crazy—not to mention his fans! But you know what? If he did it, he might actually find some peace and joy in his life." She added that last part tongue-in-cheek.

"How do you know he's not happy already?" Markus asked.

She shot him a look that said, *Are you kidding me?* And then she did her best Lahash impersonation explaining how her outside was a reflection of her inside, finishing with, "And my outsides look like hell."

Markus smiled and conceded her point. Then he tore the box off the desk that still sat in the middle of his living room. It was a work of art. The woodwork was beautiful, and its shape was unique. It curved as though it were custom fitted for a human torso to lean into it while doing work on it. The grain and color of the wood were reminiscent of mahogany, but it needed to be refinished and polished. There were some scratches on the sapele inserts at the base of the metal legs as well. Kate could not imagine where Markus found this item or how much it had cost him, but she admired his taste.

Kate fell asleep that night questioning whether she had made a big mistake career wise. On a personal level, it felt right. Not so much because it might change him, but because she had dared to say it. Too many times she had interviewed people and thoughts had come to her mind that she should say, but she didn't for whatever reason and usually regretted it later.

Beep! Beep! Beep! That awful noise intruded on what had finally become a peaceful sleep after tossing and turning for hours. If that weren't obnoxious enough, a traffic accident had clogged the artery of her morning commute. All she could think of was getting to the café for her morning drink.

When she arrived in the lobby, she could already hear Mozzella's vocal acrobats and was glad to be her customer. She looked just as happy to see Kate as she approached.

"Mornin', Miss Kate! Mozzella sho is happy to see you. Glad you ain't locked up in some dragon lair or something. Ha! Taylor done scared me, talkin' about some priest of Satan you had to go talk to."

"You mean Leif? Yeah, he's an enthusiatic fan of that priest of Satan. Maybe I should be worrying for your safety at work!" she laughed. "No seriously, it was a little creepy. I'm not going to lie."

"Leif nothin'! When his mama pushed him outta her womb, she called him Taylor, so *Taylor* it will be with me. But if you ask Mozzella, he look more like a Elliot. And speakin' a looks, I popped *Lahash* into my phone, and I'll be darned if the devil wasn't starin' back at me. You crazy talkin' to him, girl! You put Mozzella in a room with that ugly mug, and she gon' pee herself!"

Kate just laughed. She held her card out for payment, but Mozzella waived her off and said it was on the house "on account of risking your life for a magazine. You're welcome!"

Well, at least someone appreciate it. I hope Jed is in the same ballpark...or at least in a good mood, she thought. It turns out he was, but it wouldn't last long. When she entered the office suite, Jed was sitting on the edge of Jill's desk chatting with her, which was an occurrence that almost never happened. Kate got the impression he was waiting for her.

"Hiya, Kate! I see you got your usual fufu drink from downstairs. What is that anyway? Flavored milk?" He laughed and opened her office door for her.

"Good morning to you. It's a chocolate chai. How about yours? Black coffee? Bleh!"

He followed her into the office and took a seat, cheerful about their chance "coffee date." Kate saw

Jill poke her head around the corner at them just as the self-closing door edged shut. She smiled at the thought of it. Jed sat in the visitor's chair but propped his feet up on her desk as if he owned it. Well, technically, he did own it.

"So?" he said expectantly.

"What?"

"What do you mean what? Tell me more about the interview yesterday. We haven't had a good controversy in a long time, and I'm hoping you saved the juicy stuff to tell me in person. And as you know, Lahash isn't one of those dopes who try to get press attention all the time. People are going to want to read what he has to say. He's like a bad novel that you can't put down. You said you got a picture, right? Let's start with that."

She pulled out her camera and downloaded the image onto her desktop so he could see it on a bigger screen. She had to give herself credit; the picture looked fantastic. It was a great juxtaposition of the darkness man can possess and the light of nature's sun. The light seemed more intense around the edge of his silhouette, but you could still make out the deviousness of his expression and bizarre outfit.

After studying the image for a few seconds, Jed complimented her photography skills, and then as if that had satisfied him enough, he shot her a big smile on his way out the door and told her to send him the transcript as soon as it was finished. She breathed a sigh of relief since she was anxious to get started on it. The sooner it was out there for all to see, the sooner she could get a feel for the reaction and know if her job was in jeopardy. If it was, the only thing that could play in her favor for taking such a risk was if Lahash were to do something publicly that appeared as though he were actually taking steps to change his life. Deep down, she knew that was highly unlikely and toyed with the idea of leaving those comments out. However, as she replayed the audio, it was clear to her that she should print it all. And she did.

It went first to Jed for review and then to production. There was still three days before this issue was printed and distributed. After it left her outbox, there was about an hour of silence. Every time the phone rang, she expected to be summoned to Jed's office. The waiting was killing her, so she decided to try getting in touch with Joss Fenton again. Maybe she could shed some light on the reason Lahash had called for the interview and what his follow-on comments meant. If nothing else, it was her last hope of trying to find an explanation to any pushback she might get.

The line rang only once before the receptionist stated she had reached Ms. Fenton's office. By sheer luck, Joss happened to be there, and the call was connected.

"Joss here." Despite her use of first name only, she sounded all business today.

"Yes, hello, Ms. Fenton. This is Kate Owens at *What Pops.* How are you?"

"I'm good, Kate, how are you? I apologize I never got back to you yesterday. We had a lot going on around here."

"No problem. I'm calling again for the same reason. After your interview came out, we received a request for an interview from Lahash." She paused to see if there was any reaction to that. None came, so she continued. "He wanted to set the record straight—his words—about something you said and gave us an hour of his time yesterday."

"Interesting. What did he say?"

"Well, I wondered if you could help me make sense of it. Do you know him at all?"

"No. Never met him," she said matter-of-factly.

"Hmmm, that is interesting. I asked him what it was all about, with regard to you, and all he said was, 'I'm still alive.'"

"He didn't elaborate? Did you ask any follow-ups?"

"Yes, I asked what he meant by that, and he didn't really add much except that somebody will figure it out someday. Honestly, I thought we'd spend most of the time talking about that—setting the record straight, but that was the only mention of it. Any thoughts? My boss is going to want more answers. He was expecting a controversy, not some cryptic message that nobody understands but him."

"Well, keep me out of the controversies, please! As for what he said, I... uh, honestly, I have no idea what that's about. It's very strange indeed."

Kate felt somewhat let down. "So you've never worked with him or had any contact professionally in any way?"

"He's never been a client, I know that. And I can't think of any events we both may have been at that carry any significance. He performed at an award show I did some work on, but we never had any interaction. Sorry, I know that doesn't help much."

"Okay, well, if you happen to read the article and anything pops out at you, can you do me a favor and let me know?"

"Of course. Have a good day!"

"Thanks, you too."

Kate was disappointed at the dead end. She decided to quash her anxiety and seek Jed out rather than wait to be called into his office. Once she was sitting in front of him, her fears were confirmed. He started out by saying he didn't know where to begin.

There was an uncomfortable silence that lingered while he stared at his computer screen. The screen was turned away from her, but she knew he was reading the transcript. She was going to start off by apologizing for being so bold but resolved to wait for him to begin. Finally, he turned to her, leaned back in his chair and crossed his ankle over his knee. His elbows rested on the armrest and his fingers interlaced, with the pointer fingers coming together to make a steeple. He looked at her evenly, as if he were a father figure about to say *I'm disappointed in you.* The lines etched in his mature face seemed deeper than usual, and his lips were pursed. He had deep-blue eyes that were kind, but also piercing.

"Kate, we don't get interviews like this very often. I've been running this magazine for thirteen years, and when a request like this comes along, I get excited. Now I don't know why Lahash came to us or what message he intended to put out there, but what I do know is that we are not an advocacy group. If he wants to live on the edge and do things you or I disapprove of, that is his prerogative. We are not in the business of saving people or making them out to be demons that need to see the light. If I remember correctly, my last words to you yesterday were to go in with an open mind, no agenda, period. Your only ambition should be to ask interesting questions, discover something about them the public doesn't know, and apart from that, let them worry about what they do with their life.

"Having said that, let's talk about the positives here. You got a great photo of him, and we're going to put it on the cover. It will get attention at the stands. The childhood story was depressing, but new information nonetheless. It gives us a little insight into his past and what has informed his character. I'm glad you got him to share that, especially the twin thing. For not having a lot of time to prepare, you did a good job.

"My concern here is that he makes this statement that he's still alive, but you never quite got to the bottom of that. Readers are going to wonder what that is all about. And then there's the part about you challenging him to change who he is. On the slim chance that he took that seriously, he could do several different things: He could ignore it altogether, which is the most likely scenario. He could pull some stunts publicly in order to poke fun at us, or the most remote option would be to do what you suggested and shock all of us. I'm assuming he will brush it off as insane"—he eyed her to drive home the point—"but we don't know until this has had time to circulate and simmer a little while. I almost feel like we need to do a follow-up interview down the road, but I doubt he'll agree."

Kate felt chastened and apologized for putting him in an awkward position. But she explained that he didn't seem offended at what she had said but appeared more amused than anything. Trying to lighten the mood, she added, "If nothing else, I managed to make him laugh. That's a feat right there." But Jed reminded her that laughing doesn't come through on magazine pages. This final pronouncement stuck in her mind.

The next few days felt like a month to Kate who was anxious to see the final product of this month's edition of *What Pops*. The first set to print was always delivered to the offices of the writers who contributed and to the boss, of course. When it came, Kate seized it and reread every word of her contribution. She had written a brief introduction that set the scene and gave a description of Lahash; it was set apart in larger print with the picture she had taken next to it on the left. Below was the transcript of the interview verbatim. At the bottom of the second page, there was a postscript added in small font. It read, "Note: The challenge directed at Lahash by Ms. Owens was said tongue-in-cheek, and they shared a good laugh over it." She figured that was Jed's addendum to save face if they received any pushback. So be it. The cover was the picture of Lahash in the hotel with the headline reading, "Lahash: His Past, Present, and Future?"

Over the next few weeks, not a day went by without someone commenting on her interview. At work, there were e-mails, office visits, even Post-its left on her car windshield. Somebody even left a plastic halo taped to the top of her office doorframe like a miniature white basketball hoop, which Kate immediately ripped down. She was going to throw it in the trash but opted instead to keep it in the desk drawer with Lahash's file. The reactions ranged from incredulity to admiration. Some of her colleagues called it her best work yet and predicted that it would boost sales. Others were not so generous. She could tell what they thought of it by the way they smiled at her in the halls and lobby. The disingenuous smiles were paired with eyes that shifted away from hers. The opinions she cared about were already given to her. First Jed's, then Markus's, and even Leif 's opinion was solicited.

The day after the magazine hit the racks, she was down in the lobby getting a midday drink and snack, and Leif was working. She asked him to join her at a table when he had a lull in customers. He hurriedly finished up the mini rush and found an excuse to hang out by her table, so they could talk. He was excited to hear firsthand what Lahash was like, and he wasted no time in bringing up the tattoo question. He had read the article and was intrigued by the response to the tattoo inquiry. Even though Lahash didn't give a direct answer about what it meant, he had implicitly said that there was meaning behind it, which was significant enough to say he would only share it with someone he was well acquainted with. Kate regretted that she hadn't been able to get more information about the tattoo, but at least she hadn't totally let Leif down. She questioned him about his overall impression of the interview.

"As a former Hasher yourself, what was your takeaway from the interview?" she asked.

"I'd have to say it was the story about him being a twin and how his parents kind of put the blame on him for their loss. It explains some of his more bizarre lyrics. Like one song says, 'I've got an arsenal of weapons and I've used them all. My tongue, my nails, my pen, and don't forget the amniotic fluid. My victims drown, cry, writhe, and bleed. It's all the same to me.' I just assumed the reference to amniotic fluid was drug induced. Crazy stuff either way."

"And what did you think of my...questions?"

"A better question is what did I think of your statements. Telling Lahash that in actuality there is nothing rare about what he does was pretty bold. And I think you made reference to him being demonic at least four times. That may be true, but most people never say it to his face. I think he probably got a kick out of it. Seriously, I wish I could have been a fly on the wall in that room to see and hear his reaction to that. It's just not the same reading it."

"Well, I can't do anything about the visual, but if you want to hear the audio, come up to my office on your break. I'm in suite 301. I'll let you listen to the recording."

"Seriously? Wow, I'd love that! I'll be up there in about two hours. Cool?"

"Yep. It would be even cooler if you brought me my regular. I'm sure I could use a beverage by then."

"Okay, chocolate chai it is, with one shot of bribery. Done!" He laughed as he walked back to the counter.

Exactly two hours later, Jill buzzed Kate's office to inform her that her "visitor" had arrived. She paused before saying the word *visitor* as if she couldn't decide which word to use for him. Kate regretted that she didn't know Leif's last name because otherwise she would have said, "Please escort Mr.—to my office." Jill always escorted guests to the respective offices when it was someone she thought was important. To people she didn't care about, she would just point them in the right direction, and her attention stopped there.

As promised, Leif had a piping hot cup in his hand for her. In return, she handed him the recording device primed right at the beginning. He sat in the chair and listened with rapt attention, giving her varied looks and comments throughout. She relished this instant feedback. He thanked her profusely when he finished listening, and then rushed to leave after having gone ten minutes over his break time. He made some comment about "the hot redheaded receptionist" as he was preparing to leave. Kate replied, "Redheads don't date other redheads. And besides, she's not right for you. Believe me!" She felt the need to look out for her barista.

On the media front, Kate's interview garnered some attention in the usual places, mostly Hollywood outlets and the twitter world. It got about eight seconds on the local news channel, which she only knew about because her friend Fran e-mailed her the link. She wasn't sure if she liked her name being out there, especially when she was ridiculed. It sparked a flurry of media bits on Lahash, and she became tired of hearing his name. At first, she scoured the information world searching for any clues from him in the aftermath of the magazine release, but now she just wanted to go on with life and forget about it.

♟

Markus was a good distraction. He enlisted Kate's help in getting back into shape. They began running every night together. His reasoning in partnering up was that they would motivate each other. He also made it a game to see who could find the best running path; each night, one of them would pick the starting point, and at the end of the week, they would both choose their favorite. Kate loved running on the beach because of the extra effort the sand required, but Markus bemoaned all the weirdoes they constantly encountered there. He preferred to go up in the hills and run dirt trails.

One night, they were on one of Markus's paths leading up into the hills Kate was winded and dehydrated, so she gave in and walked instead of trying to meet his pace. When Markus reached the crest of the hill, he stopped and waited for her while pretending to crack a whip. After she caught up, they began to talk about work. Kate was feeling restless and thought she might search for another job. She loved writing and she enjoyed working for Jed, but she had become apathetic about that particular position. Celebrities were just not that interesting, and gossip rags were plentiful. She had felt a pull to try breaking into the news world.

"What do you think? Can you see me as an investigative journalist? " she asked.

"Hmmm. No, you don't fit the criteria. You're not self promoting enough and you definitely don't have the right opinions—or should I say, 'left' opinions."

"True, unfortunately. Maybe I'll go back to school."

"Ha! That might indoctrinate you to the predominant campus thought, and then you could walk right into a news column in today's cultural abyss. Good plan. On a serious note though, what you really need is a change in your personal life. Go find yourself a good man, get married, and have kids. That will fix your career doldrums."

She gave him a questioning look. This was the first time he had broached the subject of her single life.

"Don't worry, I'm not suggesting you try it with me! I could almost see the panic in your face just now. No, I'm giving you a nudge to do what is a natural progression in life. You've done the career thing, and even if you continued to work, you'd be so preoccupied with real life that you wouldn't notice how stagnated your writing career is. Maybe it would inspire you to write a book, who knows. But look at you, you go to work and then come home to an empty house, rinse repeat. Thank goodness I'm here, or you'd lose your mind!" He often laughed at his attempts to be funny. She found it funnier when he got mad that she didn't laugh when he thought she should.

Looking out at the city, they watched it change from dusk to evening. The lights glittered, and there was a cool breeze that dried the sweat on Kate's face. She finished off the rest of his water bottle since hers was empty, and they ran back down. Going downhill reenergized her, and she beat him to the car. That night, she conceded in her mind that Markus might be on to something. She didn't like to admit it. Here she was, telling Lahash to try doing the normal thing, when maybe it was she who would benefit more from taking her advice. Her life was selfish in the sense that everything she did was for her own benefit. Self-interest was a good thing because it tends to improve your life in a variety of ways. Nobody can claim to have zero self-interest if they are educated and have a job, and life is going reasonably well. The problem was being self-serving without an interest in anyone else's welfare. That was essentially what she accused Lahash of, but maybe she was a more acceptable version of the same thing. She resolved to find a service project that she could involve herself in.

Growing up, Kate had been involved in a church which provided never-ending opportunities to serve other people. As young as eleven years old, Kate was babysitting kids, delivering food to neighbors, and doing yard work for the widows on her street. As a teenager, it got more involved. She helped renovate an abused women's shelter with her youth group. They had spent an entire Saturday pulling weeds, planting flowers, washing windows, and painting walls. On several occasions, they went door-to-door asking for food to stock a local food pantry. She arranged garage sales to raise money for a family whose house had burned down. Her family had participated in an effort to keep local parks free of litter. At the time, she grumbled and wished she were doing other things. But looking back, she realized what a great life's lesson it was. It was during that period of her life when she felt the happiest and most confident. Her later teen years were spent experimenting with alcohol and giving into peer pressure from her more popular friends. It was on the cusp of this epoch of her life that she joined the military and broke from her family and church. It hadn't been a conscious break on her part, but her need for independence was growing. Her parents were always there in the background but never made a real effort to keep her close. They decided she was an adult at that point and pretty much let her be. She didn't fault them for it, but she vowed to never be like them in that regard. Jed and Deborah were the kind of parents she wanted to be. They were engaged in their kids' lives and never missed an opportunity to praise them and express love.

One year, for Jed and Deborah's anniversary, they had purchased tickets to spend a week in Hawaii. Kate had dropped them off at the airport. Two days later, she bumped into Jed at a grocery store. He detailed to her the events of that day they were supposed to fly to Hawaii. Minutes before boarding the plane, their eldest daughter called in a panic because her husband had suffered a mild heart attack. He was a young healthy guy, so it was a shock to everyone. They wanted to keep him in the hospital for more tests, and so Jed made the call to skip the trip and spend this time of hardship with his daughter who was also pregnant at the time. He said, "Hawaii will always be there, but my daughter's trust and reliance on me won't." Kate would have hugged him if it hadn't been inappropriate. She could not imagine her dad doing the same.

It was moments like that that gave meaning to life. Kate tried to recall the last time she had sacrificed something in order to help another person. It had been a while.

That Sunday, she made arrangements to attend church with Markus and his sister. They belonged to a small nondenominational Christian church. During the sermon, the pastor told them to ponder the story of Joseph and Potiphar's wife. He didn't go into the details of the story but used it as a jumping-off point to discuss the many forms of temptation. Kate couldn't remember the story and recalled, Lahash's quote that an educated person knows the Bible. She made a mental note to go home and read that story. When the service finished, she approached the pastor and asked him what charitable efforts the church was involved in. She wanted to be of service in some way but didn't know where to start. He praised her attitude and guided her toward a wall with a large message board titled "Outreach and Uplift." On it, there were handwritten notes requesting prayer or help in some way and printed lists of community projects that needed volunteers. She scanned them over, but nothing really jumped out at her. Markus suggested she wait for something to find her. "When a need comes along that only you can fulfill, you'll know it. In the meantime, I think it would be nice of you to bring your neighbor some peanut butter cookies." That was the one thing she could cook better than Markus. He had said it sarcastically, but to his utter surprise, she did it.

Monday morning started the same as every other Monday. Kate sat at her desk and checked her calendar to see what lay ahead for that week. She had an appointment with a well- known designer to be enlightened on the up-and-coming fashion trends; she was scheduled to have lunch at a new restaurant that a British pop star recently opened, and the chef was going to regale her with the boss's favorite dishes. The one appointment she looked forward to most was what she and her colleagues called the "posh walk." The magazine had connections with several real estate agents extraordinaire, who when selling the property of a celebrity, would let them come have a tour before it sold. It was purely for business. When the house appeared in a celeb magazine, it garnered interest in the public and presumably potential buyers. It was free advertising for the agent and an "inside look" for the writers; it was a win for both parties. Kate loved doing the posh walk. It was fun to see these fabulously expensive homes, and it was an easy write-up that the readers loved. The homes typically remained furnished throughout the showing process, which was always interesting. The taste in decor said a lot about the person living there and sometimes spoke louder and more truthfully than the actual owner of the home would if you were to interview them.

Suddenly, an instant message popped up on her screen. It was from Celeste, a quirky intern whom Kate had only spoken to once before. The message read,

CELESTE. Did you see the headline out of Florida today? The devil wears loafers.

KATE. No, what's that all about?

CELESTE. Lahash in a "monkey suit." I'll e-mail the link.

KATE. ?? Thanks!

Kate clicked on the link in her inbox. It took her to an article with the headline "Singer Lahash Brandishes Business Suit." In the brief two-paragraph article, she learned that Lahash had appeared on stage over the weekend wearing a dark-blue suit complete with a white shirt, red tie, and black dress shoes. He had forgone his usual makeup for a pair of spectacles, and his hair was slicked back into a tight bun. The article stated that after a mixed reaction from the crowd, the singer screamed something inaudible and then proceeded to strip off his attire, leaving nothing but a mesh tank top underneath and a black rag fashioned into a diaper, laughing as the crowd tore his suit into shreds. The writer ended with, "This gimmick seems to be mocking the recent interview with *What Pops* magazine" Kate wondered if there would be more of this to come.

Searching online for the Florida concert, Kate came across a YouTube video posted by a concertgoer sitting near the front of the stage. He captured Lahash casually strolling onstage. One hand was in his pants pocket and the other was swinging lazily. He looked like an entirely new person. The crowd was at first stunned into silence, and you could hear the guy recording it say "What the!" along with others in his vicinity sounding similarly confused. He kept the camera on Lahash, who just stood center stage staring out into the audience. He adjusted his tie, checked his watch, and just stood there as the rumblings from the crowd got louder and louder. Then he hushed them by asking, "How do you like my new gig?" into the microphone. Angry shouts erupted from all sides. He raised his hands to quiet them again and sang a line from one of his past hits. The band didn't join in and stripped down like that his voice actually sounded decent, but the noise from the audience drowned it out before long. People were booing, and someone even launched a wallet chain inches from Lahash's head. He dodged slightly and then slowly shook his finger in the direction it had come from. And then without any precursor, he screeched like an animal into the mic. He said words, but she could hardly make them out. As if on cue, the drummer started pounding out a beat, and the lighting changed to a single red spotlight on Lahash. He untied his hair and head banged to the beat of the drum. As the cheering reached a crescendo, Lahash ripped off the suit, popping off the buttons as he did so. Each piece he removed was hurled into the crowd. The video clip ended with two teens ripping the pants apart among a throng of people jumping up and down, and the sound of Lahash laughing in the background.

Kate sat back in her chair and crossed her arms. This was the first public reaction from him. In a way, she was amused by it. Another part of her wanted to respond to him, but she wasn't sure how. The answer came later that day.

Celeste had approached Jed with an idea. She wanted to use the Florida stunt as a way for the magazine to turn the conversation back to Lahash, putting a positive spin on things from their perspective. She had already typed up a column in which she, on behalf of the magazine, takes ownership of the incident, writing:

> In an interview in last month's edition of *What Pops* magazine with Lahash, my colleague, Kate Owens dared to challenge this rock star's self-described "rare" authenticity. In today's entertainment world and in the culture at large, we seem to be short on counter-traditional rebels who take their appearance and behavior to the fringe for shock value, right? Not quite. Entertainment media is swimming with these types.
>
> Lahash is unique in some noteworthy ways. He created a sound that is completely his own and unmistakable when it is unleashed on the radio waves. His popularity was meteoric with his first album release, and even with a lull in new music, his fans are still fervent in their support. There is no question that Lahash is a success story in the world of edgy rock.
>
> So what prompted the recent image remake at the Orlando concert? The interview, no doubt,

was what played through Lahash's mind when he planned his opening act. He laughed at the suggestion that one such as he ought to try something more shocking than creepy tattoos and man-glam makeup. He may have thought he gave this magazine a good poke in the eye. But what his behavior reveals most is that Ms. Owens got to him. Never before has Lahash donned a business suit, much to the relief of the most ardent Hashers out there. He did it simply because my colleague was right—straight arrows are the real rarity in the entertainment business. And were he to become one, it would be the most shocking of all.

Clean-cut, honest, decent family men display true daring today because they have the courage to swim against the tide of self-indulgence and tawdry charades. They work hard for the benefit of their family, and their success comes in the form of happy, productive lives. Changing your look is one thing; changing your life, from the inside first, is quite another. From a fledgling intern, that is my two cents' worth. From all of us here at *What Pops*, we wish Lahash a long and crazy life just as he is.

Jed's initial reaction was to flat out reject this idea. However, Celeste was proving to be quite remarkable and had promise to go on to have a lengthy career with the magazine. He didn't want to discourage her from speaking up when she had an idea. The problem was that he felt uncomfortable promoting any one lifestyle over another, particularly one that ran contrary to that of most of the people the magazine highlighted. He wasn't sure he wanted to take it in that direction. It would mean a shift in what they had traditionally done.

"But it wouldn't have to," Kate said after Jed shared these thoughts with her. "This is a special case. Lahash could continue to do stuff like this and try to make a mockery of me, and by extension, the magazine. Or we could print Celeste's article and get the last word, so to speak. And I promise, I will never do anything like that again."

"You better not! I admire your principles, but you 're working for the wrong company if you want to drive that tack. And I like you, Kate. You do great work. Besides, the concert thing was minor. I think it's best if we just ignore it. Printing this could cause a war of words that we don't want."

"Print it, Jed. If we get a backlash from Lahash or any kind of negative impact, I'll resign. If I leave, the controversy leaves with me."

He stared at her as if he couldn't believe what she just said. "Have you considered leaving before this?" He looked hurt.

"No. Well, not really. I toyed with the idea of getting into the news business, but that was mostly because I was worried my job was in jeopardy over this interview."

"I see," he said more to himself. "Well, I'm going to go out on a limb here and let you and Celeste have your way. This goes against my better judgment, but what the hell. I'll put it in the cue for this month."

Kate thanked him. She appreciated his willingness to take chances. Although she felt a twinge of sadness because she knew this article wouldn't be ignored, and the chances were good that she would have to follow through with resigning. She reasoned with herself that she'd wanted a change anyway, and this would give her a push to do it. Plus, there was something exciting about taking a stance on something in a public way. The opposite would be to make a written apology for offending anyone who supports drug use, promiscuity, and deviant behavior—worded much more diplomatically, of course. That was what people expected you to do, and that was why she had been ridiculed in some places. Many people had said or written something that offended someone else and found themselves groveling at the feet of the lowest in society to make recompense for saying something that was true in the first place. She had a newfound respect for Celeste and went to tell her the news personally.

Celeste worked in a small office with two other interns. She was a petite thing with bleached-blonde pixie hair and green eyes. She wore thick-rimmed glasses and bright-red lipstick. Her style was a cross between Ani Difranco and Reese Witherspoon. Kate invited her to join her for a drink in the lobby Starbucks.

Kate ordered her usual, and Celeste asked for a double-shot cappuccino, triple the foam, and caramel drizzled over the top. *That's unusual. If Leif was working, I'm sure he'd call it "special,"* Kate thought. As if reading her mind, Celeste turned to her and said, "I'm picky. I change it every time just to keep them on their toes." Then she dropped two bucks in the tip jar and gave a two-finger salute to the new girl at the counter.

Once they were seated, Kate told her Jed was going to print the article. Her face showed surprise and happiness all at once, and then she squealed a tiny laugh. Turns out she had bet the other two interns he would print it. They both predicted it would wind up in the waste bin of overambitious intern ideas, so they bet high. She was now two hundred dollars closer to buying an airplane ticket to Seattle to visit her brother.

"Congratulations! I'm glad I talked Jed into it. If I had known that, I would have asked you to pay for my drink," Kate joked. "Maybe he'll hire you permanently and promote you to my position once I resign."

"What? Why would you resign?" Celeste asked in astonishment, putting her drink back down without taking a sip.

"Because I offered to, not *if* but *when* your article causes Jed grief. I took a taboo scenic route during that interview with Lahash, and so far, Jed has tentatively backed me, but he wasn't happy about it. And we're already getting slammed in social media for being an 'activist magazine' that mocks the people we cover, yada, yada. I'm okay with leaving though. Really, since that day, I've been thinking about doing something different. I interview these people and then write up a bit for the magazine, but... I don't know. Maybe I've lost my spark."

Going home that night, she wondered what would bring that spark back. She climbed in bed and prayed for the first time in a long time. She asked for nothing more than a sense of peace about possibly leaving her magazine career. Having no other job prospects in her back pocket, she was scared and a little mad at herself for not planning this out better.

♟

It was Sunday night, and Kate sat at her kitchen barstool reading and rereading a letter she had received from the office mailroom on Friday. It hailed from a company in New York that she'd never heard of. It mentioned her interview with Lahash, calling it "exactly the kind of work we have our sights set on. "Apparently, some producer was in the process of pitching a cable television show about social influence, and they were currently doing invitation-only interviews for journalists who would help shape the show. The details were scant on purpose; a show with an influence campaign had to have a tight lid. There was a phone number to call if she wanted to come to New York for an interview. Once accepted, they would book the flight and an all-expense paid weekend in the city for a certain date. If she were hired, work would commence right away. It was intriguing, but she had so many questions. Since she couldn't call right then, she did the next best thing and walked next door to discuss it with Markus.

There was music coming from Markus's door, and she could hear talking inside. She hesitated but knocked anyway. Markus opened the door but just poked his head out rather than inviting her in. Before she could say anything, he let her know he had company at the moment but would come over to her place as soon as he could.

Kate was bewildered. Markus never had visitors apart from family. Then it dawned on her that he had mentioned a potential client coming to look at the antique sapele wood desk. But she could have sworn it was supposed to be last week.

Two hours passed, and Kate had about given up on him and gone to bed, but then she heard a light tap on the door. Markus came in all smiles.

"I have something to talk to you about. But I'll wait. You first," he said.

"Okay. Read this!" She thrust the letter into his hand and waited for him to finish. She watched him as he read and realized that he was dressed up— well, dressed up for Markus, which meant a crisp Guayabera and his nice jeans.

"Wow, that's interesting. It's not every day you get invited to an interview. Are you going to do it?"

"Of course! It's a weekend in New York and a job prospect. I don't know if I'll take it, but I'd love to hear more about it. What do you think? Wanna go to New York with me? I could use a travel buddy. I've never been there."

"Nope, New York's not my cup of tea. Don't get me wrong, I'd take a weekend trip with you anywhere else. But I hate the big city. It's dirty and crowded."

"And you live in LA. "She gave him a questioning look that exposed the irony.

"We have better weather here. And besides, I used to live in New York, remember? I hated it!"

"So what! Come with me. I'm going to need someone to tell me I'm crazy after they offer me the job and I say I'll consider it."

"Call me," he said, giving her a wink. "I'll tell you that over the phone and then convince you to come back and continue being my neighbor. I need your advice on women."

"Is that a segue to another topic?" she asked.

"Yes, actually it is. Good, eh? Speaking of women, I had a date tonight."

"Achh! And I interrupted it?"

"You did, but it's fine. It actually helped me, I think. Girl next door, good friend, competition you know how women are."

"What?"

"Joking. Anyway, her name is Jennifer, and she bought my desk last week for her swanky office downtown. Paid almost double what I paid for it. When she came to pick it up, I was cooking, and the aroma had her swooning. She couldn't believe I was a bachelor and actually cooked. So I offered to cook her dinner sometime—"

"Oh, I thought I was the only girl you cooked for!" Kate interjected, feigning hurt feelings.

He laughed. "You are usually, but if you want to keep it that way, you'll have to marry me." Not waiting for her to respond, he continued, "No, seriously I didn't expect her to accept. She's a little out of my league, if you know what I mean. She's got money and she's gorgeous. I offered to cook her dinner more rhetorically than anything, but she said yes, and here we are, eating dinner at my place tonight. It went well, if you're wondering."

"Why wouldn't it? How well are we talking though?" "She asked to meet again." He looked at her as if waiting for her approval.

"Oh, cool!" Kate couldn't understand why she was feeling jealous. She thought of what he had said earlier about women and competition, and she smiled despite herself. Hoping for a no, she asked, "Did you kiss her?"

Markus looked embarrassed to say it, which confirmed that he had. He gave a nod and then held up his thumb and index finger as if to say just a little bit.

Right then, it hit her that maybe Jennifer was the reason he didn't want to go to New York with her. And then again, maybe Jennifer was the reason Kate, resolved to go there and seriously consider moving. Markus was a good friend, the closest that she had locally. If he were to get into a committed relationship, they would inevitably lose their friendship. Although she would be happy for him, it would leave a hole in her life—socially and emotionally. However, his comment that she'd have to marry him for him to keep cooking for her did not go unnoticed. Of course, it could have meant nothing, but Markus rarely said anything he didn't mean on some level. It was one of the reasons she liked him. He didn't throw words away uselessly.

The next day, Kate called the number on the letter first thing as she got to the office. Her interview was scheduled for Thursday morning a little over two weeks from now. The lady on the phone had been cordial but unable to answer any questions outside of travel arrangements. She would be staying three days in the event a second interview was needed. That was perfect; she would be taking three days off right after Celeste's article would hit the shelves.

Over the next two weeks, things at work went on as usual. Jed had approved her time off. She didn't tell him why she was going to New York, but he had a gut feeling it was about a job. Reluctantly, he started giving more responsibility to Celeste, who was eager to take it on.

Markus had gone on several more dates with Jennifer, which Kate pretended to be interested in when Markus felt the need to talk about it with her. She could already feel their friendship becoming more distant, and it only made her look forward to this trip even more.

As she began to pack her bags, her phone started buzzing incessantly. Thinking it was Markus, she ignored it. Then she felt guilty and decided to check her messages to see what was so important. Maybe he had got into a fight with Jennifer and decided to go to New York with her. But the missed calls were all from Jed. *He knows I'm leaving. What could he possibly need right now?* She wondered. The first message only said to call him. The second one told her it was urgent. The third one said he would drive over to her house if she didn't call him back soon. So she dialed his number.

"Kate! Thank goodness! Why do you own a cell phone if you don't answer it?" He was clearly irritated.

"Sorry, I've been packing. What's the emergency?"

"Well, stop packing. I need you to cancel this trip in light of something that has come up."

There was a long pause. She didn't dare ask.

"I got a call from Oliver Weiz late afternoon, just before I left the office." Her blood pressure went up slightly at the mention of Lahash's manager. "He told me that since we continue to print stuff about him changing his life, he's going to do something about it. I don't know what that means, but he wants you to be a part of it. In other words, he wants you to do a series of interviews with him as he attempts to do what you asked him to do. I know it sounds crazy, but they are serious. And they've promised to give full access. You can take a photographer with you—"

"With me where?" she cut in.

"With you to do the interview that will happen Friday night after the show—his show, that you're invited to attend. It 's in Pennsylvania."

"What! I can't do that, Jed. I have tickets to fly to New York tomorrow morning. I can't cancel now. Send Celeste, or someone else, but I can't do it. And besides, do you really think he's going to give up his singing career and live a normal life? This is some kind of insane joke, and you're asking me to be a part of it."

"It is insane! But who started it?"

His comment offended her, but what could she say? It was true. She had started this mess, but she didn't think it would come to this. She wanted to quit right then and there.

"I shouldn't have said that, Kate, I'm sorry. Look, even if it is all a big joke to him, I want you to do the first interview at least. The company will cover your flight and accommodations. I drilled his agent about whether this was a stunt to make us look bad, and he assured me it was not. He said Lahash asked for you personally, and that he was going to give it a shot, if for no other reason but to prove to you it was useless. And if that's all it is, then fine. We can do the first interview, see what he's got up his sleeve and then drop it. He has given you a backstage pass for the show in Pennsylvania where you two will talk, and supposedly he will kick off this attempt at transformation."

"Jed, this trip to New York is for a job interview. I want to at least see what it leads to. I know I probably owe you this, but I can't reschedule." She felt bad telling him she was looking for another job, but she seriously wanted off the hook for this.

He was quiet for a moment and then said, "What if we could make both work? Pennsylvania is not that far from New York. The concert is at night, so maybe you could hop a flight down there for a few hours and then go back. Could you work it in? I hate to say it, but you do owe me this. After that, you're free to stay on as long as you need till you find another job. I know you want to move on, but please do this for me. Depending on how it goes, maybe we can get Celeste to follow up on any additional interviews, if he'll go for it."

"Why does he get to dictate the terms?" Kate asked perturbed.

"You already know the answer to that. Besides, this month's edition has only been out for a couple days, and it's already trending on social media. You've started something here that people are curious about. You said it yourself, it's a social experiment. Let's see where it leads. Lahash is game."

Reluctantly, Kate agreed to fly to Pennsylvania. The company photographer would meet her there. She had been hoping to spend that time sight seeing in New York, not hanging out at a Lahash concert. Jed had been good to her over the years though, and she wanted to leave on good terms.

4

𝓘t was unseasonably warm for an April day in New

York. The locals were savoring it after a long frigid winter, but it was a touch too warm for Kate. The humidity was just above 50 percent, which made Kate's hair rebel against the straight iron's work. Her armpits were sweaty too. She was relieved to finally reach the air-conditioned office building she had walked eight blocks to find. A receptionist took her name and then ushered her into a waiting room filled with at least ten others who were there for the same purpose. Watching them tap away on their phones and laptops, dressed in smart business attire, made her feel slightly less confident about her chances. Each interview seemed to only last ten minutes at the most. They all came out very serious looking, so it was hard to gauge the outcome.

When it was her turn, she was let in to a boardroom. There were three people seated across from her. There was a large computer screen facing her that the man in the middle operated. Each one asked her a question, and then they played a two-minute video clip for her to watch and she was asked to briefly analyze what she had seen. She felt she must have missed something because there was not much to analyze, but she did her best. They gave her no feedback. She was handed a folder with an assignment and told to return it as soon as she had completed it. Kate walked out of there feeling extremely disappointed. There was no talk about the show or what her duties would be if she were hired. She couldn't imagine why they would fly her out here for three days just to go through some sort of screening. Either way, she decided to enjoy it before she had to head back to the airport the next day.

She took a walk through Central Park, and as she passed two people seated on a bench, she heard one of them say Lahash's name. She slowed down to hear what they were talking about. The man was getting very animated, and he said, "Stop being so judgmental! What right does anyone have to mock someone's artistry? I'd rather live in a city full of Lahashes than a city full of 'straight arrows' or whatever the term was." The girl was having none of it. Kate pretended to be tying her shoe, so she could hear more.

"You're joking, right? You think a city full of Lahashes would have the decency to give up their taxi for me like that nice man did so I could meet you here? If we had a world full of men like Lahash, the human race would have ended a long time ago. And who's being judgmental? You hate the businessman, but he makes the world go round, my friend." At that, the man got up and tossed a magazine into the trash can next to them and told her to forget he even brought it up. Kate could not believe her timing. Of all the millions of people in this city, she happened to pass two just at the moment they were discussing her magazine and the man whose interview had caused her so much stress.

After a while, she sat down in the shade and opened the folder with her assignment in it. There was a group task that all candidates were to do, and then there was an individual task tailored to her. It asked her to find a bum on the street and ask him or her for help. Specifically, she was supposed to tell any homeless person that a violent man was stalking her and ask them to escort her for a few blocks. Additionally, she was to select a wealthy-looking person and do the same thing. Then she had to write in detail the reactions she received from both and write her impressions of each experience. The catch was to imply that the man following her was a government official after they had agreed to escort her.

Kate leaned back against a tree and tried to envision herself doing this. She was not comfortable with it in the slightest. Her acting skills were horrible, and despite that, she never approached strangers unless it was an emergency situation. She felt a knot in her stomach and decided that if this was what the job entailed, she would pass. She spent the rest of her remaining time in her hotel room or at eating establishments preparing for the next interview with Lahash.

Upon arriving at the concert venue, Kate was painfully aware of how much she stood out. It seemed that everyone waiting in line to get in was just a different copycat version of Lahash. She had opted to forego the business attire for something more relevant to the occasion. Notwithstanding, her gray tunic and jeans, with heeled boots and hair pulled back into a sloppy braid, she looked out of place among the concertgoers. For one, she was older than most of them, and second, she was not covered in tattoos, facial piercings, and dark makeup. Some people eyed her rudely, and others smiled and winked as if she were part of some cool club. She wasn't sure how to gain the promised backstage access, so she waited in line like everyone else.

When she reached the front where they were checking tickets, she gave them her name and showed them her company credentials. The ticket booth worker said he knew nothing about an interview, so he told her to wait on the side while he called his manager. She rolled her eyes, mostly at Jed for arranging this and then not giving her better instructions on how it would work. This wasn't something they did very often, but he should have gotten the particulars from Oliver. Nearly fifteen minutes passed before the manager came to talk to her. She explained why she was there and told them to contact the band's representative for confirmation. He explained that usually a press pass is submitted ahead of time for clearing before they could get access to a band. She was losing her patience and directed him to find Oliver Weiz right away or get Lahash himself.

After what seemed like an eternity, the manager came back and said, "You've been cleared, Ms. Owens. Follow me." She was brought to a room behind the main stage. A few people were lounging on the couches and chairs scattered around. There was a table with trays of catered food and coolers loaded with various drinks. A large flat screen displayed a live shot of the stage, which at the moment showed the equipment crew and stagehands setting up. Not five minutes after her, Matt, the cameraman arrived. Kate and Matt had worked together before on other interviews, and she was happy to see a friendly face.

"Did they give you a hard time at the gate?" she asked.

"No, not really. I knew your flight was earlier than mine, so I assumed you'd get here first. I just told them I was with you and showed them my press badge."

"How come you have a press badge and I don't?" she complained.

"Oh, sorry! I have yours. Jed gave it to me before I left because you weren't around to pick it up. They only give them out for specific venues. Haven't you used one before?"

"Nope. My interviews are always prearranged, so there's no need for additional clearance, other than showing my ID and company card to the right person."

"Here you go!" He pulled a lanyard out of his backpack with a laminated card attached and tossed it to her. "So are we doing video or just still shots? I brought both cameras."

"Let's do video, unless Lahash protests. Did Jed fill you in on the details of this meeting?" He shook his head no. "Okay, well, we might be in for a surprise. Promise me you've got my back if things get weird."

"Sure thing, boss. What's the story?" He put his baseball cap on backward and pulled up a chair next to her. She explained what had transpired since her first interview with Lahash. Surprisingly, he knew nothing about it.

"I'm sorry, I thought we worked at the same company," Kate said with an incredulous look on her face. "How is it that you haven't heard about this?

Not even after you got the assignment to fly to Pennsylvania to cover it? That's unbelievable!"

"You know us camera guys are like the ugly stepchild that's left out of everything. I guess if I read the magazine, I might feel clued in, but I can't bring myself to read it. No offense, but celebritard gossip is not my thing. Don't tell Jed that!" He laughed.

Matt was much younger than Kate. He was tall and had a strong build, so Kate was glad to have him around. She wasn't sure what kind of shenanigans Lahash had planned for her, but she couldn't shake the nagging feeling that this wasn't going to be your typical Q&A session. At any rate, she had a ninety-minute concert to endure first, so she sat back and engaged Matt in conversation about his life, work, and future ambitions. He reminded her of her younger brother Christian. He had a dry sense of humor and could hardly talk about anything without it saturated in sarcasm and accompanied by goofy expressions.

When Lahash finally took the stage, he electrified the audience. The entertainment quality of his performance was unmatched to anything Kate had seen before; although the music was not her taste, he was mesmerizing to watch. At one point, a girl from the audience jumped on stage and rushed Lahash in the middle of a song. All while still singing, he pushed her head down till she dropped to her knees, and then he turned away and the security guards yanked her off the stage. He seemed totally unfazed by it. But when he finished the song, he threatened the audience, saying that if anyone came on stage again, he would hand them the mic and let them finish the concert. It didn't happen again.

About an hour into it, Kate's jet lag was kicking in, and on top of that, the music was giving her a headache. She pulled the earplugs out of her purse and popped them in her ears. Then she laid back on one of the couches and closed her eyes. Sleep would be impossible here, but it felt good to retreat into her head for a little while. Her thoughts turned to Markus. She was trying to force herself to admit her true feelings about him, but the truth was that she didn't know for sure how she felt about him. What she did know was that she wished he had never met Jennifer. *If only he hadn't bought that blasted beautiful desk!* she thought.

All of a sudden, she felt a tug on her sleeve. It was Matt telling her she might want to hear something. She yanked the earplugs off and turned to watch the screen of the live stage shot.

Lahash was in the process of placing a chair in the center of the stage. He had a devious grin on his face. There was a low hum coming from the audience, but otherwise, it had quieted down. Lahash walked down the catwalk and began to talk.

His voice was slithery as he spoke, pausing now and again for effect. "As some of you may have heard, a woman called me a demon. Well, she's not the first. But she dared me to do something shocking—change course, so to speak. And I've decided to give her what she wants. I aim to please. But if I'm going to sacrifice this"—he threw open his arms to the crowd—"then she's going to have a little skin in the game too. Do you want to meet her? She's here." The crowd roared, but it was impossible to make out what it was collectively saying. "Come out, come out, Kate, wherever you are!" Calling to her his speech became playful, like a devious child.

Kate froze. Matt looked at her in shocked surprise. Her mind was numb for a second, and then it broke into panic mode thinking of how he wanted to humiliate her in front of a crowd of his fans. This had been his purpose all along, she knew.

"Kate! What are you going to do?" Matt asked, shaking her from her stupor.

His question made her jump. "I'm going to get out of here," she said and reached for her purse.

They heard Lahash again. "Kate, I don't like to wait. I know you're back there."

Just then, a man she didn't recognize came into the room calling her name. Before he could utter another word, she shouted that she was not going out there. He was an older man with wild salt-and-pepper hair. His beard was braided, and his ears were gauged with the holes as large as silver dollars.

"You have to! He's waiting," he said with a gruff voice.

"I don't have to do anything! That's not what I came for!" She jerked her arm away from his outstretched hand.

Matt stood in front of her and held his arms up as if to block the man from grabbing Kate. "She's not going on stage, got it? Go tell Lahash to move on with the show!"

The man walked out and slammed the door, cursing as he went. Kate remained standing; her natural response to flee was in overdrive, but she stood planted there watching the screen.

From the side of the stage, someone yelled something to Lahash. A wicked laugh escaped him. "I've been refused," was all he said. The crowd started hissing and booing. He allowed it to go on for a minute or so, and then he dropped to his knees. Just as in Orlando, a drumbeat set in and the lights went out. Strobe lights began to flash while Lahash writhed on the floor to the rhythm.

Kate couldn't watch anymore. She stormed out into the hall and called Jed. They argued over the phone for several minutes. Kate told him what happened and said she was leaving. Jed cautiously urged her to stay and follow through with the interview, but he gave her license to say whatever she wanted. Jed won. He called Matt next and told him in no uncertain terms that he was to record everything that happens and also serve as Kate's bodyguard if need be.

Still out in the hallway, Kate unloaded on Matt. The jet lag, the work stress, and these new emotions about Markus and his girlfriend were released in a verbal explosion. Lahash's taunting was the proverbial straw that broke the camel's back. She had never wanted to interview him in the first place; she didn't want to interview him now; she didn't appreciate the tactics of Lahash to bring her here under the guise of taking her advice, only to publicly make a fool of her. But mostly, she felt like she owed Jed and was therefore stuck between blowing off her job (which was the stronger pull) and staying to play games with Lahash. Matt absorbed her frustration patiently.

When the last song ended, the thundering from the crowd lasted over five minutes. The band exited the stage, and crew members began rushing around. Lahash and his three bandmates burst through the door and down the hall where Kate and Matt were waiting. Ignoring the rest of them, Kate zeroed in on the lead singer and roared, "What the hell was that!"

"Don't get so mad, pet. It was just a little entertainment for the audience."

"Screw you! Don't make me part of your entertainment," she spat.

At this point, Matt rushed to grab the video camera from the lounge and began taping. Neither Kate nor Lahash noticed. Their eyes were locked onto each other. Her anger and his initial amusement blocked out anything happening around them.

"Oh, I see! You don't want to be pulled into my world, but you seemed pretty keen to pull me into yours."

"I'm sorry that I responded to *your* request for an interview! I'm sorry that I suggested you might try something different. I'm sorry I didn't just cheer you on in your drug use and abased life like some brain-dead groupie. I'm sorry I even had to come here because my boss was catering to *you*!"

Now it was his turn to show his anger. "Well, forgive me for wanting to correct a *lie* that your magazine printed. Forgive me for being me!"

"What lie? You have yet to enlighten us. And what is your obsession with Joss Fenton anyway? You two have no connection whatsoever."

He tried to raise his voice to match hers, but it was hoarse from the concert, so it came out like a scratchy croak. "She's my sister! That's a connection!"

Kate was stunned into silence. This thought had never crossed her mind, least of all because Joss seemed sincere when she said they had no ties. Then she blurted out, "Does she know that?"

Lahash motioned to her and said, "Follow me. We're going to my trailer."

They exited through a back door and found themselves looking at a massive black RV. Before going in, Lahash grabbed a bucket of ice water sitting near the tire and doused his head with it. Then he flipped his hair forward and back again, spraying water and sweat all over Kate. She backed up and angrily wiped at her face.

Once inside, she stood there staring daggers at Lahash while Matt tried to maneuver the camera around her unnoticed. Then Lahash said, "Sit down, get comfortable. I'm exhausted!"

Matt sat down on a leather bench with a table in front of it and continued taping with his elbows propped on the table. Kate took a deep breath and sat down in a captain's chair across from the bed where Lahash had collapsed. He was wearing black leather pants, a red mesh tank top, and a metal collar around his neck. His makeup was smeared and running down his face from all the sweat and the bucket of water. Wet, black strands of hair were stuck to his face and neck.

"So? What is this all about?" Kate asked. "Why invite me here? Why this charade about changing your life?"

"I'm bored," he said flatly. "I've reached the extreme end of this lifestyle. There are no more sexual adventures to explore, no more drugs to experience, no more indecent acts to inflict on an audience, no more boundaries to cross. Talking to you opened my eyes to the banality of it all. I don't get a rush like I used to. I'm bored."

His words just hung there unanswered. Kate didn't believe him; she thought it was all a ruse to get her going. On top of that, the revelation that Joss was his sister was being tossed around in her mind. She had a million questions to ask that would help her connect this fractured puzzle of a picture starting to form. Up to this point, he had been lying down on his back with his arms and legs splayed out in pure exhaustion. But he took advantage of the silence to sit up and pull a pipe out of a drawer near the bed. She watched as he put some kind of substance in it and searched for his lighter.

"What are you doing?" she finally asked. "Please don't do that now."

"You're in my domain, kitten. If you don't like it, get out." He sounded empty.

"Okay, I'll get out after you answer some questions I really want to know. But put that way until then, all right? Remember, we're taping this." He looked up at Matt and the camera as if seeing them for the first time. Today, his contacts were a pale blue, which gave him a vampire quality. The rest of his eyes were bloodshot, and makeup had dried on his face like black tears. It made him look sad, which softened Kate a little.

"If Joss really is your sister, why would she say she's an only child?'"

"Maybe she was told that. Or maybe she does know, but it's an inconvenient little fact that she'd rather ignore, just like my parents did. Either way, I'm tired of being dead to them. Not because I've got any sentimental reason because for all intents and purposes they are dead to me too. No, I want them to face the reality of what their flesh and blood is and what their choices have been. It would be a small victory for me to shove it in their faces." His face turned hard, and the years of anger and loneliness crept out into his expression.

"*What* exactly do you want to shove in their face?" she asked, seizing the irony of his statement.

He looked at her and chuckled softly. "Ah, there it is again, Katie." She winced slightly at the kid version of her name. Her father used to call her Katie, which seemed condescending to her as a teenager. One day when she was particularly mad at him, she insisted that he call her Kate. From that time forward, she was never referred to as Katie. "Yes, I want to throw it in their faces that their son is a miserable heathen who has wasted his life on sex, drugs, and rock and roll, all while taking on a demon persona. There. I've said it. Happy now?"

He sounded sarcastic to her, but he was unintentionally making her point. She decided not to underscore that. Instead, she asked, "Don't you think they already know who you are? I mean, your life isn't exactly a secret."

"We've had zero contact since I was thirteen. Do you really think they've followed my career? I've never met Josslyn, so maybe I could excuse her for never seeking me out. But I know about her life." He met Kate's eyes as he said it, and she could see pain just under the surface. "She's worked a few shows I've played at. Our paths have crossed several times. Do you know what it's like to walk past your flesh and blood sibling and they have no idea who you are? And then I hear her talk about her parents and the great childhood she had. Aahhh." His eyes wandered off and glazed over. He cursed under his breath.

Kate thought back to her conversation with Joss. She had spoken fondly of her parents. How could these be the same two people who birthed Lahash? In a way, she wanted them to know too. She wondered why they had treated him the way they did—that is, if what he had told her about them was true. Setting that aside for the moment, she said, "My boss sent me here because he was convinced by Mr. Weiz that you were going to try to change your life in some way. He said you wanted me to bear witness of your first steps in that direction. Was that a lie?"

"Not exactly. What I said earlier about being bored is true, although I don't know that what you suggested is really plausible for me." He laughed softly to himself. "Can you really see me doing the normal family guy thing? What a joke."

"Yeah, it is a joke. I mean, who would think that you were capable of loving someone or of doing something other than performing for a bunch of zombies? No serious person would choose a family over drugs and fame, right? I heard somewhere that your stage name means 'demon that thwarts divine will' and I think you've chosen the right name for yourself. Congratulations." The sarcasm was there, but there was no edge to her voice. She was looking at a man who saw no hope for himself, and rather than digging himself out of life's rut, he chose to decorate the hole and revel living as a subterranean creature. She didn't begrudge him fame or fortune, but she did feel like the way he achieved that was a waste of human potential. Out of nowhere came a thought which she shared with him. "You can never know happiness or joy until you've suffered pain and misery. You've been on one side of that coin too long, my friend. If you ever decide to go in the other direction, it would be joyous to behold."

Lahash gave her a disdainful look and then proceeded to look for his lighter. Matt shifted uncomfortably. As soon as he lit up, she took that as her invitation to leave. She looked at Matt and pointed to the door with her thumb. He grabbed his equipment and followed her out. Lahash just closed his eyes and took a drag on the pipe. No more words were exchanged.

As Kate and Matt walked out of the stadium, she bemoaned the fact that she didn't have time to catch her flight back to New York, which was where her flight back to LAX would originate. Matt suggested changing her itinerary to match his, so they could ride back together, but she had left her luggage in a storage room at JFK international. She decided to drive with him to his hotel and get a room of her own; in the morning, they would return the rental car and catch a shuttle to the airport where she would hopefully be able to get back to New York before she missed her flight home.

While they were driving to the hotel, Matt asked her something she had been trying to answer in her own mind: "Why do you care about this guy? I mean, does it really matter to you if he continues doing what he does?"

There was a long pause before she answered. Then finally, she said, "You know, I didn't think I cared until the words came out during that initial interview. It's strange how just putting something to words can make it take root. I shouldn't care what happens to him, but I have to admit I am empathetic to the lack of parental support he's dealt with all his life. What are the odds that someone can have a childhood so devoid of familial love and then go on to be a healthy adult who love themselves? It is possible. Maybe it just takes someone pushing them in the right direction, or not even that, maybe it just takes someone caring about them to be enough. These musings of mine go beyond Lahash. It's not so much about him, although he happens to be the focus of my theory. It is pretty ridiculous, I guess." She waved her hand as if brushing aside the whole topic.

"It's not ridiculous, just not something you encounter often. It made for an interesting day, I'll give you that." He laughed.

By the time Kate got checked into her room, it was almost midnight. She wanted to shower, but she had no change of clothes. She decided to do it anyway, hoping that the steam would somehow freshen up her clothing as it hung on the outside of the shower curtain. The hot water felt good. She stood there relishing the clean feeling and the steam swirling around her. The hotel shampoo smelled like coconut; the scent always reminded her of the beaches in California. Her mind traveled back there. Now that she had pretty much blown her interview for the new job by not completing the assignment, she knew she would remain in California. And she wanted more than anything to have Markus in her life. She realized that now.

Earlier when Lahash had reflected on his life, she had hoped that he wouldn't turn it back on her. The truth was that her life wasn't all that admirable either. If family relationships were any measure, she wasn't doing so well. On the upside she reasoned that she had served her country and was a good citizen who lived by the rules of society. It sounded so sterile to her when she thought of it like that. More and more, she recognized that life was about family and relationships. This life becomes meaningful when we share it with those we love. Our parents, siblings, and friends enrich our lives, and much of what we do revolve around those people. Having children is the ultimate trial and blessing; she knew that even without having done it herself. Her childhood, juxtaposed to that of Lahash, was ideal, yet now in her adult life, she only spoke to her family members once or twice a year. Seeing the pain and emptiness in Lahash's face today made her long for a better relationship with her parents. It also made her long for a family of her own. She promised herself that when that time came, she would love them and make them feel like they were the most important people in the world. Every child deserved that.

Early the next morning, Kate found herself awake even before the alarm clock sounded. She couldn't believe how alert she felt after only sleeping a few hours. It was probably due to fear that she'd oversleep and be left stranded in Pennsylvania. With almost two hours to go before she had to meet Matt downstairs, she decided to grab something from the continental breakfast and come back to the room to eat while she watched the news. Wearing the same outfit from yesterday felt dirty, but she had no choice. She made herself a hot chocolate and snatched a half-frozen blueberry muffin. Back in her room, she got comfy on the bed and clicked the TV on. The local channel was giving the weather—a nice seventy-five degrees today. She tried finding the national news, but her channel surfing netted nothing but commercials and *SpongeBob* cartoons. Going back to the local channel was better than that, she decided.

About ten minutes into the daily rundown, the morning news show host said something that jolted her from her wandering thoughts. He reported that following his concert last night, Lahash had been rushed to the emergency room at a hospital in downtown Pittsburgh. Ox, his drummer, had found him unconscious and called 911. No other details were given, except that the cause was rumored to be a drug overdose. Kate's mind flashed back to the pipe he had been smoking in his RV. What had been in that pipe, she wondered. The report ended the segment by saying that they wished him a speedy recovery and hoped that his family might steer him toward some help. "Who is going to help him? Ox?" she asked out loud to the man on TV.

Five minutes later, she was knocking on Matt's door. He was still buttoning his shirt when he opened the door.

"'You're early. What's the rush?" he asked.

"Did you hear the news?'"

"What news? I've only had time to shower so far."

"Lahash overdosed last night, and he's in the hospital."

Matt's eyebrows rose in surprise, and he asked how serious it was. She said she didn't know, but she wanted to go find out.

"What? We have a plane to catch in less than three hours. We don't have time to go to the hospital. Plus, what makes you think they'll tell you anything. You're not family."

He was right. The hospital wouldn't tell her anything, let alone allow her access to a celebrity who just overdosed, especially if they knew she worked for a celebrity gossip magazine. She thought for a moment and then pulled out her phone.

"Are you doing what I think you're doing?" Matt asked.

"You guessed it. I'm going to call his sister."

"Hold up!" Matt said, snatching the phone from her hand. "You can't just drop this bomb on Ms. Fenton when she probably doesn't even know that he's her brother. You might want to think this through before you do that."

Kate got irritated. "What is there to think through? The man could die, and his family wouldn't even know. She's going to find out one way or another. Why not now?"

They stared at each other—her eyes communicating that she intended to follow through and his communicating that he had reservations. He shrugged and shook his head, then handed the phone back. "It's your call. I'm leaving for the airport either way in about thirty minutes."

Kate returned to her room, opting to have the conversation in private. The only phone number she had was Joss's office, and they were three hours behind. On top of the time difference, it was Saturday. She wracked her brain trying to think of how she could get Joss's personal number. That would be tricky, but she knew Jed could do it if anyone could. She dialed his number, knowing that he'd be sleeping. She listened to the phone ring over and over again. Just when she thought she had reached his voicemail, she heard a groggy "Hello."

"Jed, are you awake? It's Kate."

"Well, I am now!" he growled.

"Sorry to wake you, but I need your help. After the concert last night, I missed my flight back to New York. So I'm here in Pennsylvania and I need to get a hold of Joss Fenton. Do you think you could get me her personal number?"

Reminded of last night's events, Jed became more alert. He rubbed his eyes and sat up, placing the pillow between his back and the headboard for support. His mind ran through all the possible scenarios that could have made her miss her flight, and then her question finally caught up to him.

Slightly befuddled, he asked, "Joss Fenton? Why do you need her number?"

"She's Lahash's sister, Jed. He told me last night. And now he's in the hospital because of a drug overdose, and I think his family should know."

"His sister...what?" Jed sounded confused and irritated.

"Yes, his sister. She may not even know it, but if he dies and she finds out after the fact, it will be tragic. I need to get her personal number, so I can let her know. I have no way to find his parents, so she's the only family member to alert. She's it. Do you think you could get it?"

Jed took a moment to think of his contacts and acquaintances and then told Kate he'd get back to her. She was hopeful that he would come through. In the meantime, she would say good-bye to Matt and call a taxi to take her to the hospital.

Walking through the main entrance of the hospital reminded her of the time she had spent two nights in the Hollywood Presbyterian Medical Center after being injured in a car accident. She had suffered a concussion and some internal bleeding but would ultimately walk away from it unscathed.

Jed and Deborah had visited her in the hospital. They urged her to notify her parents, which she finally did. When her dad heard the news, he assessed the situation and found it not to be too serious, and then passed the phone to her mother. Her mom's first question had been about the car and whether her insurance would cover the damage. Then she said, "We'll pray for you, honey. Get some rest." Neither of them showed any interest in coming to visit her or offer assistance beyond prayer, which Kate had known beforehand and was also the reason why she had been reluctant to call them in the first place. She wondered now, as she waited in line at the information desk, whether Lahash would be angry for calling his sister. Assuming he would be less pleased if it were his parents, she brushed that worry aside.

When she approached the desk, she explained to the lady that she was here to visit a friend but didn't know what room he was in. When asked for the name of the patient, Kate said Lance Ashton. The lady searched her computer for several minutes and then told her there was no patient listed under that name. Kate decided to take a chance and in more of a whisper, said, "His stage name is Lahash. Can you search that name?"

The lady pushed her keyboard back and looked Kate square in the eye for the first time. "And who are you?" she asked. Kate could already see her conjuring up her training on how to protect the privacy of celebrity patients.

"Like I said, I'm a friend. I was with him last night before the incident." Kate could see suspicion written all over her face. "My name is Kate Owens."

"I'm going to have to check on that. Please step aside. There's a waiting room around the corner," she said while motioning to her right. She watched Kate wander in that direction and then helped the next person in line. When there was no one else to help, she placed a phone call. Kate watched her nod her head a few times and then look in her direction. After she hung up the phone, she waived her back.

"I'm sorry, ma'am. I cannot give you any information on this patient. There are no visitors allowed. If you'd like to leave your name and number, just in case, I can make note of it." She handed Kate a sticky pad with the hospital name and address on it and a pen. Kate ignored it momentarily and asked if they were allowing family members to see him. She responded curtly that if any family members arrived, she would let them know. Seeing that she would get nowhere with this, Kate scribbled her contact information on the sticky note and then decided to go find something to eat and wait for Jed's call.

She found a little café with a few tables near some windows. She ordered a hot chocolate and a bagel and sat down. She watched a mother with a screaming infant in her arms walk down the hallway as if some unseen force were moving her forward. Her face seemed totally unaware of her crying baby, and Kate wondered what tragedy must have befallen her. After sitting for what seemed like an eternity, her phone rang. Finally, Jed was getting back to her with Joss's cell number. It was a small miracle, he had told her, and so she owed him one—again.

Kate felt the need to rehearse this news before placing the call. It wasn't an everyday conversation. *Hi, Joss, I have something to tell you,* she thought, *and you might not believe me, but hear me out. Did you know you have a famous brother? No, that's all wrong!* She practiced a few different iterations and then decided to just call and say whatever came to mind in the moment.

As the phone rang, she glanced up and thought she saw Oliver walking around the corner. She jumped up and followed the man a few paces, but then she realized he had a stethoscope around his neck—wrong guy. Kate heard a hello on the other line, and for a second, she forgot who she had called.

"Hello?" the voice said again.

"Umm, hi. Oh, I'm sorry, is this Joss Fenton?" Kate asked, remembering the purpose of her call again.

"Who is this?" Joss asked warily.

"This is Kate Owens from *What Pops* magazine. I'm sorry to call your personal phone. I got your number from a client of yours who happens to be friends with my boss, Jed Ewing."

125

"I see. Usually I don't give my personal number out, so I'm assuming they passed it on for a good reason?" she said it in a lighthearted way, but she got her point across nonetheless.

"Yes, it's a good reason. At least I think so. I'm not sure how you'll take it." She was starting off all wrong, she thought. Joss made a *hmm* sound, indicating that she was listening. Kate started, "You told me once that you were an only child—"

"Yes," she cut in, affirming the statement.

"Well, last night, I was with someone who claimed to be your brother." There was no response, so she continued. "And now he's in the hospital. I thought maybe you'd like to know." There was a long pause, and she could hear Joss inhale and exhale before asking what his name was.

"His name is Lance Ashton...otherwise known as Lahash." Kate closed her eyes, waiting for the reaction.

"What? Why would he say that?" She seemed totally baffled by this news. "I think I would know if he was my brother! Kate, this is...I don't even have the right words for how bizarre this is. Really! What does he want from me?"

"I know, it sounds outlandish, but he says you are his younger sister—obviously—and that your parents gave him up when he was thirteen, before you were born. His description of your parents is nothing like what you described, so I'm not sure what the story is, but I believe him, Joss. Right now, I'm at a hospital in Pennsylvania where he is being treated for a drug overdose, and I can't get access to him. This isn't about a story anymore. At least it's not about the magazine. I'm resigning soon. It's about his story...and yours apparently." She wasn't sure how all of this was going to work itself out, but deep down, she was hopeful that Joss wouldn't completely shut the door on this turn of events in her life. She wanted to discover the missing pieces of this family's story. Not only had curiosity gripped her, but it also felt personal in a way she couldn't explain. As a Christian she had always believed that the human race was one big spiritual family, related to one another as children of God. And in that sense, this brother of hers, Lahash, had been wronged by his parents in so many ways; their decisions had impacted his whole life in a way that put him on a path he may have never wandered down if they had just loved him. But that was where the big question mark remained. How could they have loved their baby daughter and given her a completely different life after abandoning their son? It made no sense to a rational person. Kate wanted to know those answers, if not to satisfy her own curiosity, at least to help him find some closure. Joss could serve as that bridge, if she was willing.

They sat in silence on the phone while Kate pondered these things, and Joss, for her part could only think of asking the two people in the world who could explain this to her. She wanted to hang up as quickly as the thought occurred to her, but she didn't tell that to Kate. Finally, she simply said, "I need to think about this. Thank you for letting me know." The phone clicked, bringing the conversation to an end. Kate wasn't sure what to make of Joss's reaction. She would have been interested to know that at that moment, Joss was calling her parents to find out the truth.

5

*T*he sun was just about to dip below the horizon.

The last of its rays were coloring the dark thunder clouds purplish around the edges. Kate stared out the airplane window, exhausted from the last twenty-four hours. She had left the hospital and gone directly to the airport where she flew to New York to pick up her weekend bag and then managed to get on a same day flight back to LA. Knowing that Joss wasn't going to just pick up and fly across the country to meet her at the hospital, Kate did the only thing she could. She went to the gift store and purchased a card. There were no cards that adequately suited this situation, so she bought a get-well-soon card and scratched out those words.

Underneath them, she wrote, "Live better." On the inside fold, her note read,

> Lahash,
>
> I came to the hospital, but to no avail. They wouldn't let me see you. I wanted you to know that someone cares. And forgive me if I overstepped my bounds, but I called Joss and told her that, her brother was in the hospital.
>
> I hope you make a full recovery.
>
> Sincerely,
>
> Kate Owens

Kate left the card with the information desk lady and told her to make sure it got to him. Then she called a taxi to take her to the airport.

Arriving back at her condo was a welcome comfort. She vowed to avoid airports for at least a year if possible. After showering and putting on her most comfortable lounge clothes, she climbed in bed and fell fast asleep. She dreamed that night that she was onstage at a Lahash concert, only he wasn't on stage with her. She was bound to a chair, gagged, and sweating profusely. There was a sea of ugly faces staring at her, waiting to be entertained. In the front row where she could decipher what they were doing, a man and woman were pawing at each other in a gruesome way; the man was licking her face, and her eyes were rolled back showing only the whites. Kate started to gag, not only from the cloth that was jammed into her mouth and tied behind her head but also from the hideous scene before her. She woke up gasping for air and damp from sweat. Checking the clock, she realized she had been asleep for almost nine hours already. It was almost 6:00 a.m. Since she had worked all weekend, Jed was not expecting her to come to work today. She was disappointed that on a Monday morning in which she could sleep in, she had woken up so early. Going back to sleep would be impossible now, so she decided to go for a run.

Kate parked her car at the bottom of a hill where she and Markus had done some trail running before. They hadn't spoken in almost five days. She had thought of inviting him to go running with her, but then she remembered Jennifer and talked herself out of it. Looking at nothing but a dirt trail ahead of her was invigorating. The air was sweet today. A slight breeze was blowing through the grass and shrubs, and the sun was lighting up all the shadows. There was not a cloud to mar the sky, and the birds were singing their morning call. *Markus was right*, she thought. *The weather is much better in California than back east. Screw New York!*

As if on cue, Markus came bounding down the trail in front of her. It was as if her thought of him had produced him before her very eyes.

"Good morning, fancy meeting you here!" he said jovially, skidding to a halt. He pulled the sleeve of his T-shirt up to wipe the sweat from his brow and then gave her a hug, making sure to transfer some of his sweat onto her—something that always grossed her out.

"Ugghhh! You're worse than my brother!" she said, shoving him back.

"I've missed you too. How was New York?" He smiled at her as if he knew it hadn't gone well.

"Uh, it was complicated. We can talk about it later though. I was just about to run up this hill here and let nature work its wonders on me. I need a little pick me up. What are you doing here anyway? Don't you have to get to work soon?"

"I took the day off. I had a rough weekend. Plus, James bought a new boat and he's itching to take it out on the ocean, so we're going to have a little bro time later this afternoon."

"Why was your weekend rough?"

"Um, it's complicated"—he winked at her—"but I'll tell you all about it if you skip your workout and join me for breakfast'.

"Oh man! I just got started! Why don't you run it again with me—do a little double duty? Then we'll get breakfast." She really didn't want to stop after only fifteen minutes, but she knew she could be convinced. He thought for a second and then agreed to run with her just to the lone wax myrtle up about halfway. Kate readily agreed. She was interested to find out about his weekend and to get his thoughts on hers.

When they finished, Kate followed him to a quaint little café she'd never been to before. They were seated outdoors on the patio. There was a brick fireplace in the center and potted flowers all around. They both ordered huevos rancheros and a large glass of freshly squeezed orange juice. She traded him some chunks of avocado for his extra slice of bacon. She loved avocado, but she loved bacon more. Markus prodded her to go first, but she wanted to listen while she ate, so she let him do most of the talking until the bill came.

It turns out that Jennifer, or Jenn as he called her, was the source of his troubles. Kate tempered her glee at this news with a knit brow and a few grave head shakes. She took a swig of juice every time she was tempted to smile. He and Jenn had enjoyed several amazing dates, which all ended with kisses, of course. But the kissing wasn't enough for Jenn, apparently. One night after laughing till their faces hurt at a comedy club, they decided to go for a walk on the beach. Markus had genuinely wanted to just sit and watch the waves at one point. He dug down in the sand and tried to engage her in a philosophical conversation. Nothing too deep, he assured Kate, but he wanted to learn what she thought about different things. He brought up current events and politics, two subjects she attempted to brush off as "boring." When he pressed a little bit, she did something so unthinkable to Kate she could hardly believe it. In an apparent ploy to distract him from those boring subjects, she began to undress and while flashing her chest asked, "Aren't these more interesting than the news?" Markus was appalled that she was doing this in public and told her she didn't have to do that to get him to change the subject. She told him it was the fastest way to move the conversation along, plus it was dark, so nobody would notice what they were doing. He explained that he was so turned off by her behavior that he drove her straight home that night and called it quits.

At this point, Kate was choking on her juice from laughing so hard. Markus's blood ran hot like any man, but he also had class. He wasn't going to roll her after only five dates and especially not out in the open.

"Kate, it's not funny! I was so mortified. Who does that? We aren't teenagers anymore. And besides, I don't know what's more unappealing, the fact that she was so bold in trying to seduce me or the fact that she couldn't have a conversation about anything of substance?" Markus looked seriously offended.

"Well, most men would find her boobs more interesting than the boobs in Washington," Kate spluttered, breaking into another fit of laughter.

Markus shook his head. "That's it. You're paying for your own breakfast. This was not helpful at all."

After hearing his story, she didn't want to darken the mood with hers. Messing up a job prospect (or two), missed flights, drug overdoses, and hospital visits could be discussed another time. Now that he was free of Jennifer, she decided to invite him to dinner to talk about those things later. He promised he'd try to get back from boating early enough.

Kate spent the rest of her day cleaning and running errands. She was in a great mood. Markus called later that evening to ask for a rain check; he and James had got a late start on their boating expedition, and now they had found a sweet spot for fishing and were not ready to head back to shore. It was fine with Kate. She wanted to spend some time researching jobs and then get to bed early so she would be ready to go back to work the next day.

On her commute to work the next morning, Kate was listening to the news and caught the Hollywood Report, which was a brief rundown of any celebrity news. The rest of the program was focused on national news, but she always wanted to hear the Hollywood Report because it sometimes led her to good interviews. Today, the broadcaster reported that Lahash had been released from the hospital where he had spent two days recovering from an apparent drug overdose. She wondered if Joss had heard it. Moreover, she wondered what Joss had discovered about potentially having a brother that she never knew about. Would her parents come clean? Would a contrary history emerge?

As was her routine, Kate stopped at the lobby Starbucks for her usual. Her two favorite baristas were on the bar. She chatted with Mozzella while Leif whipped up her drink. She knew they would both get a kick out of hearing that Lahash had called her out on stage over the weekend. She detailed the experience for them.

"You should have rocked that!" Leif stated enthusiastically.

"That red bun o' yours must be pulled a little too tight! Are you crazy?" Mozzella shot back. "That man had nuthin' but humiliation planned for you, girl. You did right, stayin' backstage and refusing to play that game. Mozzella knows what she talkin' 'bout y'all."

Kate thanked them and headed upstairs. She fought the desire to call Joss again, figuring that the ball was in her court. If she wanted to ask Kate for details, she knew how to reach her. However, the question of how to handle that part of the story in the ongoing saga with Lahash was tricky. She didn't want to exploit something so personal. On the one hand, Lahash did offer the information during a scheduled interview; on the other hand, Joss was brought into it without her consent. Kate sent a meeting request to Jed to discuss it. She had only met with Lahash at his request, and she knew he'd want to write about it in the next edition of the magazine. She also knew that he didn't like to make enemies in this business. Joss Fenton was not a celebrity, but she was well connected, and he respected her. Moreover, she was a person with a private life, and she was entitled to keep her privacy.

Jed had not responded to her meeting request by the end of the day. He had been busy with a director's meeting and had to put out some fires in the advertising department. Just as Kate was finishing up the last of her to-dos that day, she got a call from Jed inviting her to dinner at his place that night. He told her she was welcome to bring a date but cautioned her that they would be discussing work. Seeing that she had a rain check in reserve for Markus, the two of them made plans to go.

Kate wore an ivory-colored cocktail dress with capped sleeves and a knee-length hemline. Her dark-green gator skin heels added another two inches to her height. Her hair was wrapped up in a tight twist, and gold spheres dangled from her ears. Markus's eyes lit up when she met him at the door.

"You look absolutely stunning. Thank you for inviting me," he said.

"Thank you. And you're going to be happy you canceled last night because I was going to buy a roasted chicken from the grocery store to feed you. Jed is a much better host than I am."

Markus drove them to the Spanish-style estate that was Jed's home. They parked on the semicircle stone driveway that was lined with an array of flowers and trees. Despite knowing Kate for several years, this was the first time she had invited Markus to a social function with her boss. He was anxious to meet the man Kate spoke so highly of and his wife. Deborah met them at the door and greeted them both with hugs and a kiss on the cheek. She was always affable and gracious to her guests and knew how to put on a fabulous dinner.

They were led to a courtyard out back, where a table was set underneath a large gazebo. Small lanterns were strung around the roof of the gazebo, and the table was glowing with candles. There was a large vase of fresh pink and white flowers in the center. Next to the gazebo was a rectangular saltwater pool, flanked on both sides by a row of chaise lounges and a side table for each pair. It was quaint and fancy all at the same time. Outdoor speakers were playing a cello and piano duet barely audible above the din of conversation. After some polite small talk, Jed got right to the point.

"So, Kate, how did your interview in New York work out?" He and Markus both had an interest in hearing this. Markus had yet to hear whether she would be moving, so he stopped eating the couscous salad and waited to hear the verdict.

"It wasn't what I expected. I was given an assignment that made me very uncomfortable, to

138

say the least. It turned out to be a moot point, however, since I spent most of my time in Pennsylvania rather than New York. I never completed it, so I'd guess I've been scratched from the list of candidates. It's okay though. Coming back here just confirmed that I don't want to move. I like it here. New York is nice to visit, but I can't imagine living there." She caught Markus's eye, and he gave her a wink.

"Well, that's too bad," Jed said nonchalantly, "but does it mean you're not resigning?"

This topic made Kate uncomfortable because she didn't quite know yet. She had said she would, but she didn't have a plan yet. Sensing her hesitation, Deborah chimed in. "Well, if you want my two cents' worth, there's no need to right away. There was no serious harm done in this whole thing with Lahash. Of course, there were people who didn't like it, and you probably offended some of his fans, but readership is up and so are our Facebook followers. You just take your time to figure out what you want to do, Kate. Jed, could you grab the main course for me? It's on the platter in the kitchen."

Jed rose to grab the rib roast, and Deborah began to pass around the garlic potatoes and artichokes. Kate thanked her, and when Jed returned, she told him she would stick around for a while if it was okay with him.

"Plus, I think I have unfinished work. Don't you want to know what happened at the concert?"

"I thought you'd never ask. Of course, I want to know! I'm paying your salary after all."

"Yes, I'd like to hear this too." Markus joined in. "You haven't told me anything since you got back."

Addressing Jed, Kate said, "Well, you already know the two most unexpected bits—the concert episode and the whole sister thing."

"Wait, I missed this. What concert? And whose sister?" Markus asked. Since he and Kate hadn't talked before she left, he was unaware of her second interview with Lahash.

"Oh, that's right," Kate said. "You didn't know at the last-minute Jed asked me to fly to Pennsylvania to talk with Lahash again. He happened to be giving a concert there while I was in New York for the interview."

"Okay, now the picture is making sense. You mentioned being in Pennsylvania earlier, and I had no idea what you were talking about. Go ahead, fill us in." Markus sat back ready to listen. Jed was watching him the way a father might with a guy who wants to date his daughter. His eyes were scrutinizing his every move. Kate noticed and found it endearing. She related what had happened during the concert and afterward in the trailer. When she finished telling them about her phone conversation with Joss, she asked Jed what he wanted to write about it, if anything.

"You shouldn't print that without giving Ms. Fenton a heads-up," said Deborah.

"Do you think it's true?" Jed asked.

"I believe him. It's the only reason he interviewed with me in the first place."

"Well, we still have three weeks before our next printing. Let's hold off for now. Celeste and Sam are working on some good stuff with that Canadian actor who stars in the new detective blockbuster. We can run with that. But do what you can to put something together that Joss Fenton can deal with. We don't need her permission, but it'd be nice to get the nod from her. By the way, what did Matt get? Footage or still shots?"

"Both, I think. He was filming in the trailer. Man, I haven't even gone over that yet! I need to see him tomorrow." Kate thumbed a note into her phone.

"Who's ready for dessert?" Deborah asked. Without waiting for an answer, she brought out the chocolate fondue pot complete with a tray of fruit and tiny cakes for dipping. The candles were waning, but the four of them sat for another hour chatting and enjoying every last drop of chocolate. Markus and Deborah got along so well you'd think they were old friends. Jed was a bit more reserved with him than he usually was. Based on his line of questioning, Kate knew he must be looking for clues about the kind of man Markus was. She wondered if he'd share his assessment of Markus with her later. For his part, Markus handled the evening gracefully, and Kate was happy to have had him there.

They spent a lot of time together over the next few weeks. On the surface, their relationship was very much like how it had been pre-Jennifer, but there was a deeper feeling now. Any time the conversation hinted toward their future, Markus would say, "You never know what might happen. Keep an open mind." They never talked about it directly; it was always more of a peripheral subject. But there was a sense of knowing in certain things they said. In that one weekend where his fling had come to a sudden end and the lure of a new job in a new place had vanished for her, they both took a second look at each other.

One night while watching a movie which starred an actress that Kate was set to interview, her phone began to vibrate in her pocket. She checked the number and didn't recognize it, so she ignored it. About an hour later, the same number appeared again. She let it go to voice mail, but both times, they had hung up without leaving a message. A third time it rang, and Kate finally answered.

"Hello?" she said irritably.

On the other end, a deep voice said, "Third time's a charm, I guess." Kate didn't recognize the voice, and she sat there holding her breath trying to sort out who it might be. It was almost midnight. Silence followed. Then he spoke again, "Well, I don't know if I'm living better, but I lived."

"Lahash? How did you get my number?" Kate's heart was thumping, and she couldn't quite wrap her mind around this unexpected phone call.

"It was written on hospital paper, which was stuck on the card you left me. It's nice to know you care." His smile came across over the phone.

Suddenly, she felt stupid for writing that. "Well, I'm glad to hear you recovered," was all she could think of to say. He made an *hmpf* sound, and then there was more awkward silence. After a while, she couldn't take it anymore and gave in, asking him what he wanted.

His reply surprised her. "I want to know if Josslyn believed you when you told her about me."

"No, she seemed shocked by it. She asked what you wanted from her. I told her you were in the hospital, and that was about it. She said she had to think about it, and I haven't heard anything from her since."

"Is our interview going to be printed in your magazine?"

"I don't know yet. Do you want it to be printed?"

"Yes," he said simply.

"Why? The whole reason we ever had that second interview, if you can even call it that, was because you said you wanted to change your life. I'll admit I was doubtful, but then why on earth would you go through the trouble of making sure I made it out to that concert? Was that the lie you thought would get me there? Just to pull some stunt on stage?"

"You want to know the truth? I wanted to use you...to bring you into my world in a small way. I wanted to see you scared and humiliated. I wanted to watch you be at my mercy, with thousands of lunatic freaks watching. Then you would get a taste of what I have experienced before, and I'd see that you're just as weak as I am. Then maybe that tiny itch I had to give it all up would be scratched. I also wanted to use you for your platform. Back when you interviewed my sister, I realized that I could use you to get a message to them. You could tell my family about me in a way that I haven't been able to, even with my fame.

"Imagine that you were discarded and forgotten by the people who chose to bring you into this world. Then imagine that you hated them and hated yourself for it, and so you abuse yourself in every way imaginable. You create a character that allows you to forget who you were supposed to be. You get swallowed up in a dark world where nothing matters and become addicted to it. Then imagine

144

that you find out you have a biological sibling. You've never met them, but you hear about them through their work. They're leading a normal life. They get interviewed for the first time, and you hear that their parents—your parents—loved them and raised them as an only child. You hear that they were religious and involved in your sibling's life, when you knew them to be abusive and hateful. Then imagine that you find a link to them that can show them their hypocrisy, the fruits of their labor, so to speak. You wanted to know about my tattoo? It's a symbol of everything I've been describing. My mind couldn't comprehend the reality of this duplicity from my parents. My mind has no answer to the endless question—why did they hate me?" His voice cracked, and he stopped there.

Kate was stunned, not only by the call but by what he was saying. You think you can read a person sometimes; while you might get some of it right, there's always more there. All these years of seeing Lahash in magazines and on TV, she was only seeing him as a character, not as a person with a family and a past. Of course, that is what he wanted people to see, and watching from a distance only allows a narrow view. But tonight he was being vulnerable. He had admitted that he had an itch to change. She wasn't surprised by the "itch" as he called it, but she was surprised that he admitted it to her. And rather than asking why his parents hated him, what he was really asking was why didn't they love me like they loved her?

"How do I serve as that link?" she asked.

"Finish what you've started, kitten. Write what I've told you. Tell my sister that *our* parents lost not one son but two. Tell her I've watched her career from a distance, mostly out of sick curiosity. Tell her I found out about her when I was twenty years old. At that time, she was two years old. My aunt, the one I was sent to live with when I was thirteen, found a way to get a message to me. She knew the mother of my old bandmate that died and told her that if she ever saw me to let me know I had a baby sister named Josslyn and that my parents had moved to a new state. I guess she knew I'd never hear it from them. Blaine's mom eventually tracked me down through some friends and gave me the message."

Kate cut in before he could go on. "What was your reaction to that news?"

He took a breath and exhaled slowly through his teeth "A mixed bag...I guess. I felt pity for the helpless baby. It was hard to believe, to be honest. But it was also liberating in a sense. I knew that door was shut to me, so I shut it right back. It's like those hotel doors that connect two rooms that you can open on either side. Well, we both locked them after that and threw away the key. I celebrated the news by snorting a bunch of coke and singing a eulogy to my parents at the show that night. That became somewhat of a tradition." He chuckled to himself, but there was no mirth in his voice.

"Okay, I'll write it. I've never written anything like this before, not for the magazine anyway. It feels too personal to be in a layout next to ridiculous fashion trends and Hollywood gossip." *It feels like the wrong venue altogether*, she thought.

"It is what it is. Have a good night, Kate."

She hung up without saying anything else. *That felt too personal too*, she thought.

The days that followed left her agonizing over what to write. At work, she ignored everything else, sometimes sitting there for hours and only getting a sentence or two down. There was still no peep from Joss. This made it easier for her to do it justice by Lahash and focus less on what Joss might think of it. She hadn't told anyone about the phone call except for Markus. He assured her that whatever she wrote would serve the purpose. But always the voice of reason, he cautioned her that she had only heard one side of a three-pronged tale, and she shouldn't be too harsh on his parents or paint Joss in a negative light.

When the article was finally finished to Kate's satisfaction, she sent it to Jed for review. She purposely waited for the run-up to the printing deadline, just in case he decided not to print it. Then she could reason with herself that it was just submitted too late and not because of the content. Of all the pieces she had written for the magazine, this was the only one she felt invested in.

147

6

$\mathcal{T}$he week was coming to a close. Kate and Markus had planned a weekend hiking trip in Yosemite. Although she was anxious to go, she lingered at the office, waiting to hear back from Jed about her final article on Lahash. She had gone through Matt's photos from the concert night in Pennsylvania. He had managed to capture raw emotion that conveyed more than anything she could conjure up in words. In the initial hallway encounter after the show he had snapped a photo of her railing against Lahash for calling her out on stage. Her back was to the camera, but you could tell she was worked up, from the hardness in her frame and her pointed finger aimed squarely at Lahash's chest. He stood in front of her with his hands tugging on either side of the small white towel around his neck, his head cocked back in a defiant smirk. One of his bandmates was passing around them coming toward Kate. He was giving her a sideways glance and wiping sweat from his brow. In another photo was Lahash lying back on the bed in the trailer, propped up on one arm. He was sweaty and exhausted looking, but he was staring out the window clearly lost in other thoughts. His expression was sad. Kate looked at herself questioning him and wondered what she was saying in that moment. Her eyes looked pleading; her hands were both open with the palms up and she was leaning toward him. She found it amazing that Matt had managed to set up the video cam on the table and maneuver the camera as well in such a tight space. She had yet to view the video footage, but the photographs were exceptional and all she really cared about anyway. Her three favorites were selected and sent with the article.

Kate sat there staring at her computer, wondering if Jed would ever get back to her about whether he intended to publish it. Suddenly a knock came. She jumped up and called out, "Come in!" It was Jill. Kate's disappointment was written all over her face when she saw the receptionist enter her office.

"Expecting someone else, clearly," Jill stated. She stood there awkwardly with her arms folded.

"Yeah, sorry, I'm waiting for Jed. What is it?"

"Is Lahash still a subject of yours? I mean, will he be in the next issue?"

Kate thought this was a strange question coming from Jill. She didn't usually involve herself in the magazine's content, particularly not anything Kate was working on. "Uh, yeah, that's what I'm waiting on. Jed is reviewing a piece I wrote on him. Why?"

"I just heard that he's been checked into a local hospital."

"Really? What happened?"

Jill shrugged her shoulders and shook her head. "I'm not sure, but a friend of mine who works at the hospital just tweeted about it."

Kate's mind was racing. She had to confirm it herself. "Thank you, Jill. I appreciate you telling me that." Jill nodded and opened the door to leave. Before she left, Kate added, "And, Jill, if your friend tweets anything else about him, will you let me know?"

"Yep," Jill called over her shoulder.

The Internet was up, and within seconds, it had confirmed that Lahash was indeed in the local hospital. Kate marveled at how fast news traveled these days. There were no specifics given, but one headline intimated he'd had some kind of heart failure. Other comments were jumping to the conclusion that he'd had another drug overdose. In either case, she didn't want her article printed anymore. She didn't want to appear to be taking advantage of his personal crisis. She picked up the phone and called Jed, hoping he was still in his office. After getting no answer, she tried his cell. Still no answer.

With Jed missing in action, Kate decided to call Joss and let her know what was going on. If the article hit the shelves just days from now, she wanted Joss to know that she tried to stop it, given Lahash's current situation. On a more selfish level, she also wanted to know if Joss had come to a conclusion either way about her famous brother. This would be the perfect excuse to contact her again and find out. Fortunately, Joss was in the office that day.

"Kate, it's good to hear from you again. I've been putting off calling you, but now that I've got you on the phone, I'd like to see if we can meet sometime. My whole world has kind of flipped upside down with the news you gave me."

Joss had broached the subject before Kate did, which was a relief to her. "So it's true then?" Kate asked, just wanting to confirm it before she said anything else.

"Apparently so. I didn't want to believe that my parents could have kept that from me my whole life, but their initial reaction to my questions about it told me the answer. They are actually flying out here soon, so we can discuss this in person. It's not a conversation they wanted to have over the phone, ya know?"

"Of course. Well, I am looking forward to talking with you. When will your parents arrive?"

"In about two days, actually. They've held off telling me anything until they get here, but they promised they would tell me everything. Depending on how that conversation goes, I wondered if you could facilitate a meeting with Lahash. I'm not even sure if he'd want to meet with me, but I've got to hear his side of the story. This has been keeping me up at night. I still can't believe it. All those times I had seen him on TV or at various events, he seemed so..." Her voice trailed off as she thought of the right words.

Kate jumped in, "He seemed so different from you? Yes, I know. But I haven't told you what I called about yet." She took a deep breath before continuing. "I heard on the news this morning that Lahash is in the hospital again. This time he's local. I'm not sure what happened, but this might be a good time to reach out to him." Kate could tell that when Joss responded she had covered her mouth with her hand. Joss agreed to meet her at the hospital and see if she could at least find out what his condition was, even if she didn't speak to him in person.

Kate thought how strange it must feel to be confronted with a situation like this. It's one thing to find out you have a brother whom you've known about—the entertainer, that is—but never knew he was your biological brother. It's quite another thing to discover that your parents kept this big of a secret from you and then only divulged the truth when they were forced to.

Before leaving the office, she printed out a copy of her article. She wanted to give Joss a preview and get her thoughts on it. She left a message with Jill to let Jed know where she was and to tell him to hold off on sending her article to print.

The two women had agreed to meet at the floral shop on the ground floor of the hospital. Joss was standing in front of a large cooler gazing at the colorful bouquets inside of it when Kate arrived. She was dressed all in black except for a bluish-gray scarf wrapped loosely around her neck. Her hair was in a side braid that hung almost to the crease of her elbow. They greeted each other and moved to a sitting area to talk.

Once seated, Kate told her about the article she had written and about how it might be printed soon. "I've been trying to reach my boss to cancel it ever since I heard Lahash was in the hospital, but so far, I haven't been able to reach him. It may be too late anyway. If production already has the layouts complete, it will be impossible to replace it with something else. I didn't want you to think that I was taking advantage of this situation"—she gestured at their surroundings—"by coming out with it now. It's just the way the timing worked. And it is personal in the sense that he's very open with his thoughts about your parents. I brought you a copy, so you could read it. He asked me very explicitly to convey his message. I'm not sure *What Pops* is the best venue for it, but he insisted that I use my platform to write it."

Joss was listening intently and asked, "Was the message intended for us? His family? Or for mass consumption?" Kate noted her use of the word *us* when referring to his family. Clearly, she had accepted it.

"Mostly for you and your parents, but he doesn't care if the world hears it."

Joss reached for the article in Kate's hand and began to read. Kate watched her eyes as they scanned through each line. She was trying to detect the emotions coming through them, when all of a sudden, her phone rang. "Markus! I forgot!" Kate said to the phone before answering it. She stepped away from earshot to talk.

When she came back to where Joss was sitting, she started to explain that a friend was waiting on her to leave on a weekend road trip, but she stopped short when she caught a glimpse of Joss's face. Her eyes were red rimmed, and her chin was quivering. "This is awful," she said. "He can't be talking about my parents. They aren't this way, Kate!" A tear sped down her cheek as she spoke.

"I'm sure they aren't now. But is it possible that they were like that in the past?"

She shook her head. "I just can't imagine it. My mother was so tender with me as a little girl, and my father's form of discipline was sitting me on his knee and giving me a stern talking to. Even as a teenager when I started to make dumb decisions that disappointed them, my parents were always so loving and forgiving. They often said they prayed for their other children that hadn't joined our family yet." She stopped there and seemed to be searching her brain. "I always thought they were referring to children they hadn't had yet who were still in heaven. They are pretty old, and every time they mentioned praying for their other kids, I would tease them about being too old to have more children. But I longed for a sibling. Being an only child is great in one sense. You get plenty of attention. But when they were busy, I always wished I had a brother or sister to play with." She sat there covering her face with her hands and resting her elbows on her knees.

Kate unbuttoned the jacket of her dress suit and sat back down. She placed her hand on Joss's arm and said, "I know this is hard. But your brother wasn't given the kind of childhood that you were given. He's here in this building somewhere though, and I think we should find out why—how serious it is, I mean. It would be good to know, especially with your parents coming to town." She gave her arm a small encouraging squeeze. Joss rose and approached the information desk. Oddly enough, they didn't question her claim of being the famous singer's sister. The hospital employee discreetly wrote down the room number on a Post-it note and pointed them to the west-wing elevators.

As they walked down the hallway to his room, Kate sent a text to Markus that she was going to be a little longer. She hated to put off their trip, but she knew Joss would never do this on her own. She was as anxious about this visit as Joss was, only for different reasons. They walked in silence until they stood outside the door of the room where he was lying. Then Joss turned to her and started to ask if she'd go in first, but before she could say anything, Kate called out to someone.

"Mr. Weiz! Is that you?" A man sat further down the hallway with his head resting back on the wall and a cup of coffee in his hands. Upon hearing his name, Oliver Weiz raised his head and gave them a tired but surprised look. He was wearing slacks with a gray dress shirt, but his tie had been pulled loose and was hanging over one shoulder. His hair was disheveled, and bags were forming under his eyes. He looked different from when Kate had first met him, but she couldn't mistake that tan skin and salt-and-pepper hair.

Oliver stood and shook hands with both women, giving Joss a curious look. "Pardon my appearance," he said. "It's been a rough twenty-four hours." He tossed the Styrofoam coffee cup in the nearby trash can and ran his fingers through his hair.

"What happened?" asked Kate. Then she remembered these two had never met and made the introduction. Oliver nodded at Joss and said, "I know who you are. I'm not sure why you're here though." His face was questioning, and Kate filled him in on what his client had revealed to her the night at the concert. He looked at Joss in a completely different way and seemed to be working it through his mind. If he found it unbelievable, he didn't say so. Then addressing them both, he stated that everything about this hospital visit was off the record; they both readily agreed, and he proceeded to relate the events that had brought them there.

"The night before last, the band was scheduled to appear at a private gig in Malibu. I typically don't accompany them to shows or social gatherings, but I help arrange them. This particular one was of interest to me because of reasons I won't discuss, but I went early to the location and was taking care of a few things before they arrived. People were starting to gather, and the evening was revving up, but the band hadn't showed yet. I couldn't reach Lahash, so I called Ox. He told me that Lahash was acting strange and didn't want to go. I reminded him that they were being paid to be there and in no uncertain terms, told them to drag him there if they

158

had to. About two hours later, they showed up, but I could tell something was wrong with Lahash. He looked awful—puffy eyes, lethargic. He started talking gibberish. I assumed he was on something, and so I shoved him into a bathroom to splash some water on his face while I got him some coffee. Not that that would help much, but I couldn't think of anything else to do. I didn't want him to completely make a fool of himself and ruin the night. As it turns out, the night was ruined, but it wasn't because of drugs like I thought. When I returned to the bathroom with a cup of coffee, Lahash was crumpled up on the floor, moaning and bleeding profusely from the bridge of his nose. He must have fainted or something and hit his face on the sink. He's pretty bruised now as well. Anyway, we got him to the hospital, and they ran a bunch of tests and they've discovered that he's in stage four of kidney failure."

While Oliver spoke, Kate was watching Joss's face. She had a concerned look throughout the account, and her eyebrows rose in surprise when he related the diagnosis. A thought seemed to pass through her mind which gave her a peculiar expression. Then she said, "Stage four sounds like a final stage. What's the prognosis?"

Oliver hesitated for a few seconds and then said," His condition is dire. He would probably need a transplant, but because of his other health issues, he may not be a good candidate for a transplant."

"What other health issues?" Joss asked.

"Well, he's a diabetic who doesn't eat well or take care of himself, for starters. I'm sure you know about his drug and alcohol abuse. And on top of that, he's got some other infection that they just discovered and are treating him for now. His whole lifestyle is a health issue." Oliver shook his head and glanced toward the door where a nurse had just entered the room to check on Lahash. He motioned with his hand in that direction and suggested they go see if he was awake.

When they approached the door, Kate could see that the nurse was elevating his head, and Lahash was scowling at her. His hair was a black matted mess and his face looked paler than ever, except for a cut and some bruising on his forehead. His tattooed arms looked out of place extending from a pale-blue hospital gown. They were much more suited to dark colors and rougher materials, such as leather and chains. He looked almost comical to Kate, except that she could see how miserable he was. When he looked in their direction Kate noticed for the first time that his eyes were a natural blue. She had never seen him without some outlandish-contacts and makeup; his natural look was so different. It was clear that he took those measures to change his appearance because his normal face was too pleasant to match his persona. Seeing Joss's strawberry-blonde hair made her wonder if his natural color was similar.

Joss became timid as she entered the room. Kate wanted to say something to break the ice, but

Lahash beat her to it. "Looks like my day just got much more interesting. At least now if I die, I can go out with a little drama." He directed his gaze right at Joss and waited. She looked at Kate for help.

"Well, it seems a little absurd to make a formal introduction, but I'm going to do it anyway," Kate said, forcing a smile and trying to lighten the mood. "Joss, this is Lahash. Lahash, meet Joss Fenton. "Joss smiled but found it hard to look at his eyes, which unyieldingly bore into hers.

In his characteristically mocking tone, Lahash said, "Josslyn, it's nice to finally meet you. Where does *Fenton* come from? You're not married."

In all this time of contemplating these two people, Kate had completely overlooked that incongruence. *Yes, why did they have different last names?* she wondered.

Joss smiled and asked if she could take a seat near the bed. Lahash didn't protest, so she pulled the chair up next to his bed. "First of all, I have to tell you that I'm still in shock to have discovered that not only do I have a biological brother but that it's you. It hasn't sunken in yet, so you'll have to forgive me for being so awkward. I have so many questions for you, so much I want to know! But let me answer your question first and maybe you'll indulge me with a few of my own," she looked at him expectantly.

"Oh, I'll answer those and then some. You probably won't want to hear all that I have to tell," Lahash said with a poisonous laugh. His face looked pained and distorted as he laughed. The puffiness around his eyes and the bruising from hitting his face when he collapsed gave him a ghoulish look.

Joss seemed to mentally dismiss his comment and delved into her story. "I was born Josslyn Fenton Ashton. Fenton is the surname of my godparents, Lula Jane and Albert Fenton. They were a missionary couple that befriended my—our—parents before I was born. They played a key role in Mom and Dad's conversion to Christianity, which was a pivotal point in their lives. Apart from that, they were just really good friends. They sort of embodied everything that Mom and Dad wanted to be. They were happy, intelligent, generous, charitable, and funny to boot. Mom said that they were like a torch placed in the middle of a midnight swamp. Anyway, they originally gave me Lula as a middle name but then argued that they wanted both Lula Jane and Albert to be represented, so they selected Fenton instead. On my first birthday the Fentons gave me some very thoughtful presents, and in return, Mom and Dad decided to write them into their Will as my guardians in the event of any untimely passing on their part. Furthermore, they thought that three names ending with n was redundant, so they dropped Ashton and legally named me Josslyn Fenton. I questioned them about that when I got older; I thought it was strange that they would drop their own family name and replace it with someone else's. They explained it away by saying they couldn't very well drop my first name or my middle name, given that it had been a gift of sorts to my godparents. Anyway, by that point, I was already a teenager and used to being known as Joss Fenton. After sweet Lula passed away and I became an adult, I thought about changing my name back to Ashton, but my career was taking off and Fenton Consulting had already been established, so I left it alone. And there you have it." She remained leaning forward and waited for a response.

Up until that point, Lahash remained stone-faced, with the exception of a small scoff when she mentioned that converting to Christianity had been a turning point in his parent's life. He never knew them as Christians. In fact, they used to mock the Christians who lived on their street. Their disdain for "blind sheep," as they used to refer to churchgoers, had shaped the young mind of Lance Ashton, as evidenced in both the abuse of religious imagery at performances and in the lyrics he penned. Even his chosen stage name, and the eponymous band he formed, was something anathema to the Christian God. His parents owned a small amount of intellectual property in the band because of the ideas they had once spewed in front of their son. How ironic that it was now turned against them, both on a personal level as well in a general sense. All of this was fuel to his fire, although

Joss was unaware of any of it, at least not on a conscious level.

"Interesting," was all he said in return.

"I read that you were a twin," Joss said. Her voice cracked when she said the last word.

"You read correct." His gaze turned to Kate, who was doing her best to recede into the background. Oliver too had adopted the same posture and was standing quietly in a corner of the room. Neither of them said anything.

Joss began again but stumbled and stuttered over her words. Oliver cut in and asked if they'd like to be left alone to talk. At exactly the same time Lahash said yes and Joss said no. As much as Kate wanted to hear this conversation, she also knew that she was keeping Markus waiting. She apologized to Joss and excused herself to leave. Oliver followed suit but told Joss that he'd wait outside in the hallway if she needed anything. On their way out, Kate thanked Oliver for staying and told him to call her if anything came up. Then she sped home to make her apologies to Markus; she couldn't wait to get out of the city and enjoy a change of scenery.

7

$\mathcal{T}$he trip to Yosemite had done wonders for Kate.

She came home relaxed and refreshed. Her relationship with Markus seemed to have turned a new leaf as well. They had allowed themselves to discuss work and careers only on the drive up to the park. Once there, they both agreed to leave that topic alone and focus on everything else. At first it was hard to mentally pull away from the thing that took up most of their time during the week, but it got easier as the hours passed, and the trees, rocks, waterfalls, and wildlife claimed their attention.

One afternoon, while the two of them sat on a blanket in a grassy area that had a perfect view of El Capitan, Kate caught Markus staring at her rather than at the domed bald rock. She commented that if

165

all he wanted to do was to stare at her face instead of the cliff face in front of them, then they could have saved themselves a six-hour drive. He'd replied that her face was more beautiful to him than that gray rock ever could be. His comment both embarrassed and thrilled Kate in equal measure. It also managed to remove a long-standing barrier they'd had to discussing their feelings for each other. That evening, an honest conversation was had over dinner regarding their relationship. He admitted to harboring secret hopes that Jennifer's brief cameo in his life would stir up some jealousy in Kate. She'd never admit to that, but she did concede that she was happy Jenn was a thing of the past. Kate had become so comfortable around Markus that she was caught off guard when a certain look in his eyes made her blush and feel a little exposed. His presence in her life had never made her feel nervous or self-conscious the way other men had; it was as if she'd forgotten that he was an available man with natural human desire rather than just a generic neighbor she could rely on. That realization had made the remainder of their short getaway more exciting.

Kate's first order of business upon returning to the office was to check in with Joss and get an update on her hospital conversation with Lahash. She had temporarily forgotten about it during her brief excursion, but now it was all she could think about. Had they spent hours getting to know each other? Or had it ended in disaster? Would she go back for a second visit? Was he even still in hospital? She couldn't reach her by phone, so she decided to browse the Internet for news of Lahash's discharge from the hospital. There were a few local outlets that had discovered his condition, but nothing indicated that he had left the hospital.

Skimming through the local online news outlets, she completely overlooked a message scrawled on purple stationary near her keyboard. It was from Jill, and it read, "J. Fenton invited you to lunch *today* at noon. Meet her at the bistro where you first interviewed her. Call if you can't make it." When she picked it up, she realized it had been placed there with a copy of the latest edition of the magazine. She had not seen hide nor hair of Jed since she'd sent him her in-depth write-up on Lahash, which was strange. He had never returned her messages to stay the article. Immediately, she flipped through the glossy pages, and there it was on page 6; her article, with all the emotional detail of Lahash's family story, was sandwiched between images of Britain's royal family and a story of the latest fad to hit California— transgendered spa and relaxation centers. It seemed so out of place. Furthermore, it bothered her that Jed had sent this to print and then disappeared. Thankfully, she had let Joss preview it, so there was no need for an apology or explanation as to the timing.

When she arrived at Truxton's for lunch, Kate discovered that she and Joss would not be dining alone. An elderly couple, which Kate could only assume were Mr. and Mrs. Ashton, were seated at the table with Joss. The man was leaning back in his chair with his arms folded and looked half asleep. He had a pale-blue button-up shirt on with a pair of glasses sticking out of the pocket. He was balding with just a strip of white hair wrapped around his head from ear to ear. Despite his age, he looked big and strong. The woman seated next to him, however, looked frail. She was petite and appeared to be grasping onto the table for support. Her hair was light brown with streaks of white, and it was pulled up into a tight bun in the back. She was wearing a floral dress with a white-knit cardigan over it. As Kate weaved her way between the tables to reach them, she noticed the woman whisper something to Joss and point in her direction. Joss looked up from the menu and stood to greet her.

"Kate, I'm so glad you could make it! Sorry for the short notice. Come and meet my parents, Brent and Charlotte," Joss said.

They both stood to shake hands, and Charlotte blurted out, "Charlie, call me Charlie."

"Nice to meet you both. I'm Kate," she said, smiling. She couldn't quite believe she was meeting, Lahash's parents whom she had just written about and not very flatteringly at that.

Brent cut right to the chase. "We know who you are Ms. Owens. We've been reading your reports on ...uh, on Lance." Clearly, he wasn't sure what to call his estranged son; Kate assumed that his stage name was a source of discomfort to them both. "Charlie and I have decided we'd like to talk to Joss and Lance together about our past, except Lance won't see us unless you're there." He paused and looked at her as if she had something to do with that.

Kate wasn't sure how to respond, so she just said "Oh?" and looked at Joss.

"That's true. He refused to talk to them without you present. He didn't give a reason either. When they arrived, we all tried to see him at the hospital. He knew they were coming to town because I had told him when I was there on Friday. So he had directed the hospital staff to keep them away. I couldn't see him either, and I found out later it was because they had moved him to his house where a nurse will check in on him once a week for medication and so forth. Oliver arranged that. He's been there since yesterday and Oliver has been our go-between passing messages back and forth. He's the one who finally convinced him to see us, but the condition was that you had to be there."

A waiter interrupted them to take orders. It was salads all around for the ladies and a Thai chicken flatbread for Brent.

Once the waiter meandered back to the kitchen, Kate picked up the conversation again. "Well, I'm happy to go with you to talk to Lahash"—Brent cringed at the mention of his stage name—"and I'm sorry if you feel like that's an intrusion on your privacy. I can't imagine why he wants me there, but I'll go."

"It is private, and I'd like to keep it that way, Ms. Owens. We don't need our family history blabbed about in your magazine," said Brent.

Charlie shot him a disapproving look and added, "We're grateful for your help, Kate. Without you, this fracture in our family would have probably died with us, and as uncomfortable as it is, we'd like to try to mend some of the damage that's been done." She glanced at Joss and gave her an apologetic look while caressing her arm. "I never thought this day would come. We made our choices for better or worse, and now we have to face the consequences Josslyn, honey, I'm so sorry about all of this! I hope you'll allow us the benefit of the doubt once we all have our say."

Joss gave her a brief smile and nodded her head slightly. "Mom, like I told you before, I love you both. Knowing the truth won't change that, but I do want to know the whole truth. It will help me put the pieces together and understand you better. And to be honest, I'm praying that I can establish some sort of a relationship with Lance. We've only spoken once, but I already feel a connection to him. I've literally spent hours over the weekend searching anything I can find to read about him. The Internet is replete with crazy stuff, but after talking to him for an hour or so the other day, I'm keeping an open mind."

Brent inclined his head while she talked about Lahash. Even as the topic changed, he stared out the window a lot and didn't add anything substantive to the conversation. It was Charlie who made the final arrangements to meet again later that evening when Kate got off work. If Lahash agreed, they would meet at his residence that night after dinner. Joss called Oliver to make the appointment. After confirming that Kate would be there, he asked for Kate to give him a call right back. She dialed his number as soon as he hung up with Joss, and he told her to go somewhere private.

Excusing herself from the table, she walked toward the hallway where the restrooms were. "What's going on?" she asked.

"Listen, this meeting the parents thing might be a bad idea. Lahash is in terrible shape, and he's got something devious up his sleeve. When Joss first called me about this, I ran it by him, and he flat out refused. At first, I tried to convince him to do it because, selfishly, I hoped maybe they'd snap him out of this funk he's in and it might motivate him to keep on working. He makes me a lot of money, and I'd like to keep it that way. But I pushed a little too hard, and he snapped. He did a one-eighty and talked about what a great idea it would be to expose mom and pop in front of Joss, burst her bubble, so to speak. He used to be extremely private about his past, but now he wants every sad detail out there to humiliate his parents. He wants everyone in their new life to know what they were like, which is where you come in, incidentally."

"Wait, he wants me to print this?" Kate asked surprised.

"Uh huh, and it's going to be some pretty ugly stuff from what it sounded like. Even if you don't print it, I think it's going to be very uncomfortable for everyone involved including Lahash. I think his declining health has messed with his emotions. He's sitting at home, banned from his normal substance abuse, and he's got a nurse sticking a tube in him all the time. He's miserable and looking for something to destroy to make him feel better."

It was starting to make sense to Kate now. She knew his parents were determined to see him now, but she didn't know if they were prepared for an emotional ambush. "Should I give them a heads-up? A warning?" she asked.

He shook his head and rubbed the back of his neck like he wasn't sure how to answer that and said, "I'll leave that up to you, but just be prepared to mediate if it comes to that. I'll be there too, but I'm staying out of it. I'll be working downstairs."

Kate was lost in thought as she made her way through the lobby heading back to her office. Leif made several attempts to get her attention from the

Starbucks counter but was unable to shake her from the internal conversation she was having inside her head. It wasn't until Mozzella's boisterous laugh cut through the din of people coming and going that Kate snapped out of it and looked in that direction.

"Earth to Kate!" shouted Leif as he waved his arm above his head. Mozzella was still shaking with laughter.

"What's with you two?" Kate asked as she approached the counter.

Taylor 'bout jumped outta his apron trying to get your attention! And you looking like a zombie walkin' through here," Mozzella said while imitating them both very animatedly.

Kate had forgotten momentarily that Leif's real name was Taylor. Leif offered to make her the usual, on him, if she would stay and chat for a minute. She consented and sat down with him at a table. He pulled out the latest magazine and complimented her on the article she'd written about Lahash's family.

"This is fascinating! It's not your typical *What Pops* stuff, you know? And I wanted to thank you for getting him to open up about the tat. That was something I've wondered about for a long time. So Lahash and I have something in common besides similar tattoos—parent issues! Anyway, I told a few friends of mine who are big fans of his that I knew you and they had a request. They're willing to pay for it or exchange favors or whatever. I don't know how this stuff works, but they wondered if you could get an autograph for them." Leif showed her a faded scrap of material that had been scrunched up in his pocket. He explained that it was part of a shirt his friend had worn to a Lahash concert, which he had thrown onto the stage hoping Lahash would take it. Apparently, Lahash grabbed it and chucked it back out to the audience where it was torn to pieces. The owner of the shirt fought to get it back but was only able to rip a small section of it from another guy. He had saved it as a concert souvenir and wanted Kate to try to get it signed by Lahash if she was going to see him again.

"No, absolutely not," Kate said. It's my policy to never ask anyone for an autograph, especially if it's for someone I don't know." Leif looked crestfallen. He'd had a glimmer of hope that she might say yes. Attempting to soften the rejection, she added that Lahash was ill, and it would be tacky to make such a request in his condition.

"Oh, I guess that makes sense. How did you know he was sick? Do you guys talk now?" Leif asked.

Kate had divulged in her writing the late-night phone call she had received from Lahash, which was the source of the information in her article. She felt a small urge to tell Leif that she would be going to Lahash's house later that evening but decided against it, remembering Brent's desire to keep it private. Plus, she didn't want him to press her for this favor. Kate had never asked anyone for an autograph even when she got the opportunity to meet one of her teen movie star crushes. It made her feel more like a teenybopper than the professional that she was. And in any case, Lahash was not that sort of self-loving celebrity either, who cared for flattery or the chance to make a fan squeal with joy over some memento he bequeathed to them. He'd just as soon make a fool of them.

"No, we don't talk," she said. "I just know he was recently released from the hospital for some health issues. Tell your friend I'm sorry. If I hadn't washed the shirt already that Lahash sprayed his sweat all over, I'd give you that, but it's not quite the same now that it's been reborn with lilac fabric softener." She smiled and thanked him for the drink.

She stepped into the elevator and bumped into Jed. "Where have you been!" she demanded.

He chuckled and gave her a wink. "Hiya! I see you've missed me." She just stared at him as if he knew how many times she'd tried to get in contact with him over the last week, and nobody seemed to know where he was. He could see she was not amused. "Okay, I should have at least told Jill where I was. But I have boss privileges, so I'm allowed to take an impromptu trip once in a while."

"Where were you? And why didn't you tell me you were going to print that article?" she asked.

They reached their floor, and Jed proceeded to greet people as he passed them in the hallway. Finally, he said, "One of my poker buddies has a vacation house on Catalina, and he invited us to go for a little R and R with him at the last minute. So I kidnapped Deb from work and whisked her off to an island retreat. We flew on his private helicopter, which is a fabulous way to travel, by the way. We snorkeled, went fishing, wined, and dined. It was just what I needed. Plus the layout was set—your article was great!—and things here were at a nice lull, so I jumped at the opportunity." He looked like he'd had some sun and was in a good mood, so Kate decided to lay off him and just let him ease back in to work mode before she mentioned the hospital visit.

"Well, I'm glad you enjoyed yourself. I spent the weekend in Yosemite. We didn't get nearly enough time there because of the drive, but—"

"Come with me to my office. I need to talk to you about the meeting I just came from," Jed said, interrupting her.

And just like that, Jed was back in work mode. Kate followed him to his office. He pulled a box of specialty chocolates from his desk and offered one to Kate. She bit into it, and a gooey liquid dripped out of the center onto her chin."Ew, what is this?" Kate asked, wiping her chin and making a bitter face.

"Kahlua filled, you don't like it?" She rolled her eyes and reminded him that she doesn't drink alcohol. "Not even in chocolate?"

"Not in any form. Thanks anyway."

"My apologies. Anyway, I just came from a board of directors meeting, and we had an interesting discussion. We're not like the big three, so we have to reinvent ourselves once in a while to stay alive. Well, I guess Advance and Time Warner have had their share of changes recently, but that's beside the point. What I'm getting at is that we'd like to go in a slightly different direction in the coming year." Kate could tell where he was going with this, and she had mixed emotions about it. "Your latest piece on Lahash sparked some excitement in the board and elsewhere. It seems to have turned a page for this magazine, so to speak. Adding a little depth and history to our interviews intrigues me. This latest edition was a test run, and it paid off, my dear. Sales are up, and we're generating online chatter. It was really fabulous work. You should be commended."

"I appreciate that, Jed, but remember, this was kind of a special case. The family catch was a one-off. It's not like every celebrity is going to reveal some dark family secret every time they talk to us. I don't see how we make this transition last, especially in a monthly platform."

"We don't, that's just it. We discussed moving to a quarterly and doing more research on our subjects."

"You mean digging up dirt?"

"I mean finding something more interesting to report on them than money and lifestyle. We could start doing multipart write-ups on individuals, over an extended period. Like what you've done with Lahash, for example. Do you have any follow-ups planned?"

Kate hesitated. "Well, I'll be talking to him tonight, but it's off the record."

Jed frowned. "What do you mean, why are you meeting him then?"

"I tried to tell you about this last week, but things have taken a turn with him. He was in the hospital this weekend. On Friday, I went to see him with Joss. She talked to him for the first time. We found out that he has stage-four kidney disease and diabetes, so he's in bad shape. You'll also be interested to know that I just had lunch with his parents today. They want to see him and, uh, repair the family to the extent they can, or at least make an apology or something, but he won't see them without me. I have no idea why. I've served my purpose in this scenario. I'm honestly a little uncomfortable playing this role because the father clearly doesn't want me there, and he's made it a point to say this is all to be kept private. So I'm going just to facilitate a family meeting, but nothing else." She opted to keep the conversation with Oliver quiet for now. If what Oliver said was true about Lahash planning something devious to hurt these people, she was not going to be a pawn in the game.

Jed rubbed his chin and scrutinized her face. "Does Lahash want it kept private?"

"Jed, he opened up to me before he wound up in the hospital. I doubt he wants that out there for public consumption, even if he would like to humiliate his parents publicly. And I can't tell the story of why his parents are here without mentioning his health problems. That's why they came."

"Hmm. Tell me about the parents."

"They're not what I expected. The dad, Brent, is a big guy who doesn't open up much. His wife Charlie is nice though. If I had to guess, she's the one who's driving this visit. I think she feels really bad about the decisions they've made, and she told me she's grateful for what I've done to bring this all about. I think it will be a burden off her shoulders after all these years, quite honestly. They're retired now in Loudoun County, Virginia. I think they ran a printing shop or something like that. Joss seems close to both of them. She sat between them at lunch and held hands with each of them at different points. They didn't go into their past much. They're holding off until they can say it all in front of Lahash and Joss together. Tell me something, have you made a final decision on this transition yet?" she asked, changing the subject.

"No, I'm planning an all-hands meeting with the employees to get everyone's input. The board would like to have a decision next month, so we can start reformatting and get a plan in place for next year. We may have to make a few cutbacks in the process. I'll need to have a clearer vision before I proceed."

"Okay, well, I'll let you know how tonight goes, but as far as I'm concerned, it's not work related." She stood to leave. "Don't get sloshed in here or I may have to limit your chocolate intake," she said jokingly.

He shook his head muttering, "How can you not like Kahlua chocolates? It makes no sense."

♟

When Kate got home later that afternoon, she found a white rose tied to her doorknob with a note from Markus. It read, "Sleep over tonight? Kidding! I'll settle for a late dessert. Come over at 8." She laughed to herself at his tactic but mentally awarded him some charming points. Regrettably, she would have to pass tonight. She called him and told him about her outing before he needlessly put his plan into motion. He was disappointed that his clever invitation was for naught. But he agreed to postpone it rather than cancel altogether.

That evening, Kate dressed in a conservative navy-blue top and khaki skirt. The address she was given was surprisingly not too far away, just up Old Topanga Canyon Road. They would all meet at the front gate where Oliver would let them in. She pulled her Touareg up to the iron gate where the other three were waiting. The security gate opened to a short driveway at the end of which was a very normal-looking two-story home with a two-car garage in the front and steps that led up to the front door. It was dark-tan stucco. There was a walkout balcony over the garage, and the house was set back above that. There was a tangle of various kinds of trees on either side, making the neighboring houses barely visible. It was a nice house but had none of the grandeur that many did on the posh walk tours. It was definitely not the sort of house she imagined Lahash living in. A medieval castle with dark stone passageways seemed to suit him more, but I guess those were hard to come by in LA County.

Oliver greeted them and led them into an entryway. The decor was plain, but it seemed to have a decorator's touch. It reminded Kate of a model home; it had everything a home should have, but it wasn't customized and did not have that lived in feel. She asked Oliver if Lahash had lived there long, and he told her that this was his second home, which he only stayed at when he had to be in LA. His primary residence was up in the Bay Area.

Kate looked over at Mr. and Mrs. Ashton to assess their state of mind. They both looked anxious. Brent said little while the rest of them made small talk. After a few minutes, Oliver directed them upstairs to a study where Lahash was waiting for them. He stole a look at Kate and raised his eyebrows in a questioning way. She gave a slight shake of the head to communicate that she hadn't told them about Lahash's motives for agreeing to talk to them. Just before opening the door, Oliver whispered to them that he was suffering from alcohol withdrawal and might be cranky. They all made their way into the room, all except for Brent, who lingered in the doorway. He stood there staring at Lahash. While everyone else settled into a seat, Brent remained planted. Kate could see his hands shaking. His whole frame seemed to be quaking, but you could only tell by the slightest shaking of his clothing. Nobody had said a word yet, and then the silence was broken with a sob.

"Oh, my son!" cried Brent. His voice was broken and shaky. Saying the words seemed to release him from his hold in the doorframe, and he almost crumpled down to his knees. Tears filled his eyes, but he never took them off Lahash. Charlie went to his side to steady him. Even she seemed surprised by this sudden outburst. Joss covered her mouth with her hands and looked at Lahash for a reaction. Pain was etched in her face. The sob from this large man was full of emotion—sadness, regret, and something else that was indecipherable.

Lahash was sitting on a black chaise lounge in the corner of the room. He looked even worse than he had in the hospital. His lanky frame was draped with a black silk sheet; he wore a ripped-up black T-shirt and dark-red pajama pants. One leg hung out of the sheet onto the floor, revealing long neglected toenails. His skin appeared deathly white next to the black colors surrounding it. His eyes had dark circles around them, and his hair was in ratty black tangles. He sat there motionless, staring at his father. Only the slightest widening of his eyelids gave away his surprise at his father's appearance and behavior. Kate caught it, and it occurred to her that after so many years of not seeing each other, the changes in both men must be drastic. Lahash did a better job at suppressing his shock than Brent did.

"What do you want, old man?" His voice was hard and cold.

"Your forgiveness...and a chance to explain..." His voice cracked as he spoke and then trailed off when Lahash turned his head away in disgust.

Nobody seemed to know what to do. They all just waited for Brent to continue. After a long uncomfortable pause, he spoke again.

"Son—"

"Don't call me that!" Lahash shrieked. The veins on his temples popped out, and his eyes looked wild.

His words seemed to rip through the air and smack Brent in the face.

Meekly, Joss spoke up. "Please, let him talk. I need to hear this too." Her voice was choked, and she looked pleadingly at her brother.

Lahash was breathing heavy now. His nostrils flared in unison with the rise and fall of his chest. But he crossed his arms and looked at Brent again, as if giving him the go ahead to speak. He had not looked in Kate's direction once, and she wondered what he'd expected her to do in this situation.

Brent sat down next to Charlie on a love seat across from Lahash. He was still shaking, but Lahash's rebuke seemed to have helped him compose himself and reign in some of the emotion. "Let me start from the beginning. I never told you much about my childhood, and maybe I should have. You and I never did much talking, did we?" He didn't wait for a response, knowing that none would come. "The truth is, I didn't know how to talk to you. My father never spoke to me outside of an order, and he was always angry. He left my mother when I was nine. She raised me by herself, but she never missed a chance to tell me what a burden I was. She had to work double to feed me. No man wanted her because of me. The house was always messy because of me, and on and on. She convinced me that I never wanted to have children of my own. By the time I met your mother, I was an alcoholic who had no use for family. And I told her as much.

Incredibly, she stuck around long enough for me to come to my senses and marry her. When she got pregnant six months later, I was livid. I went on a drinking binge and urged her to have an abortion. But your mother refused. She spent every last ounce of energy she had trying to convince me that having this baby would be a blessing. After a while, she wore me down, I guess. I started to rethink my views on having kids. I watched her belly grow and for the first time in my life, I started imaging myself as a father. I wondered what the baby would look like, and I liked to feel the little kicks on her stomach. We had no idea there were two of you in there." He paused as the tears started to flow again. Charlie too was silently wiping tears away from her cheeks.

Lahash found he was interested to hear this, despite himself. His ears took in every word, but his body language was conscientiously saying otherwise.

"Your mom went into early labor and was having a tough time. I rushed her to the hospital, and she spent twenty-eight long hours trying to deliver you. At one point she was getting really weak and her condition didn't look good. For the first time in my life, I asked God for help, and I wasn't even a believer at that time. I promised that if he saved your lives that I would be a better man. But then the unthinkable happened. You were born, but there was something wrong with your mother. That's when the doctors realized there was another baby there. Only he was...stillborn.

185

"I almost attacked the doctors trying to get an answer out of them as to what happened. They said the baby had suffocated in there; his oxygen was cut off or something. I didn't understand how it could happen. I was so angry! Here, I had just prayed for the first time in my life, and moments later, I had a dead baby in my hands. I let the anger blind me to the fact that I had a living son. God seemed to have cursed me, just when I was warming up to this father idea, and so I chose in that moment to reject him, and in the process, I kind of rejected being a father too. It took me many years to realize that my prayer had indeed been answered that day. Two babies never even crossed my mind. I was praying for a healthy baby and a wife to live through it, both of which, I received. Your twin brother was a test for me, one for which I failed miserably."

Brent dropped his gaze to the floor and began to rub his hands together. Lahash tried to look as though he was enduring something he cared nothing for, but still he listened.

"I took it out on you. Life was miserable for your mother, and she became jaded. She couldn't enjoy motherhood because I wouldn't let her. Eventually she started blaming you too for your brother's death. You didn't deserve that." He stopped talking and broke down sobbing. Voicing these memories was painful. He got up and excused himself for a moment to pull it together.

186

While he was out in the hall, Charlie picked up where he left off. "Lance you have every right to hate us for how we treated you. Losing that baby, as painful as it was, was no excuse for being awful parents to you. As you got older, our behavior toward you had taken effect. You were difficult and behaved badly, which is the natural outcome of being mistreated the way you were. But that only made it worse for you. The more you rebelled and got into trouble, the worse we were. It was a vicious cycle. We were a family out of control. It got to the point where we couldn't handle you. I hated myself for the kind of the mother I was, but I didn't think I could change. So I started feeling like you might be better off living away from us. At that time, your Aunt Beth was giving us a hard time about the way we raised you. She heard you'd started using drugs and insisted you needed to get away from the friends you had. Beth always had cared about you. She couldn't have kids, and so her husband left her for a woman who could. After that, she was constantly checking up on you, asking me how you were doing. She came to visit you a lot when you were younger. She even threw you a birthday party when you turned five, did you know that?"

Lahash slowly shook his head no. He listened to his mother, but he barely looked at her.

"Yeah, she traveled to Kentucky and bought balloons, cake, presents, the whole works. She didn't know any of your friends, so she gathered up some neighborhood kids to come sing "Happy Birthday"

187

and play with you. You were the happiest I've ever seen you." She smiled as she recalled the memory, but then her face clouded over again, probably over guilt for not doing it herself or for not creating more happy memories when she had the chance to. "Anyway, Beth called one time when I was particularly angry at you for skipping school for a month straight. She lectured me about keeping track of you better, and I blew up and told her that if she thought she could do a better job at raising you, then she could have at it. Without pausing to think, she said yes, and the next thing I knew, you were gone.

"It was a relief to have you gone at first. I wondered how she'd manage, and secretly, I hoped she'd be a miserable failure at raising you, just to prove a point. After a while, I realized you might never come back. If you had, I don't know what I'd have done, but being without you changed me. I had time to self-evaluate. Your dad and I no longer had you to blame for our state of misery. We were just miserable people, plain and simple. Once it occurred to me that we were the problem all along, not you, I went through a terrible bout of depression. I asked Beth to stop giving me updates on you because it was just too painful. I cut everyone off, even your dad. We hardly spoke to each other for at least six months. I literally hit rock bottom in every sense."

Brent had been listening at the door and came back in when she mentioned hitting rock bottom. Kate shifted in her chair but didn't dare say anything. Joss remained stoic. Kate couldn't tell how

188

all of this was hitting Lahash. She wondered if any of it changed his perception of his parents. When Brent spoke again, his voice was hoarse, and his expression was sadder that ever.

"Your mom would have died drinking herself to death if an angel hadn't intervened." Lahash shot him a piercing look at the mention of angels, but his dad continued. "Your Aunt Beth sent us a letter telling us that you'd run off, and she didn't think you'd be coming back. Reality set in that we'd never see you again most likely, and your mom got drunk and started tearing the house apart. She screamed at me like a madwoman, blaming me for losing both of her sons. I had to get away from her, but I was afraid she'd kill herself if I left her alone. I stepped out onto the front porch, and this couple was walking down the sidewalk. They saw me crying and heard her inside wailing, and they asked if they could help. I told them no and to leave us alone, but they were concerned and kept asking questions. Your mom heard me talking outside and ran out to see who it was."

Charlie cut in, "I thought he had called the police to come take me away." Lahash smirked at that.

"It was Lula Jane and Albert Fenton. They were taking a walk through the neighborhood and passed our house just as this was happening. And thank the Lord they did! Lula managed to calm your mother down, while Al and I had a nice long talk on the porch about family and about God and so forth. Long story short, they befriended us and got some people from their church to start counseling us. Little by little, they invited us to start making changes in ourselves. First, we started reading the Bible. Then we gave up alcohol and cigarettes. It wasn't easy, but we could feel a difference. Over the years, we've continued to change and become different people than we were back then." Brent paused and looked from Lahash to Joss.

"Ah, I see," said Lahash. "So you tossed your past in the garbage heap and started over, right? New state, new kid, new life. How nice." His expression was accusatory, as if he was daring them to agree. His eyes belied the calm posture he was trying to maintain. He added in a deep slow drawl, looking at his mother, "I do hate you, Charlotte, and I don't need your permission to." Charlie looked down at her hands and nodded her head as if she expected that.

The comment had a visible effect on Brent and Joss. Joss seemed to want to justify her parents in some way. She turned to them and asked, "Didn't either of you try to find Lance? Ever?"

"Yes, we did," Brent said. "After Charlie got pregnant again, we moved to Virginia. We vowed to be good parents, to love this baby like we wished we had loved you, Lance. We viewed this baby as a second chance from God. You can't have thoughts like that without rehashing the past. We wanted a second chance with you too, but we had no idea where you were or how you would react to us. Beth had told us you were playing in a band and were pretty involved in drugs and alcohol. We tried to get information on your whereabouts from people who knew you in North Carolina, but the only real tip we got was somebody who thought you had gone to jail.

"In all honesty, we wanted to protect Joss from the lifestyle choices you were making and from ever knowing what we used to be like. But we did want to reconnect. It wasn't until your band started playing on the radio that we realized who you were. Just by chance, I happened to see you on TV after one of your singles took off. We couldn't believe how much you had changed, but I recognized you right away. We started hearing things that you were involved in, and... uh, some of it was pretty disturbing...Um..." He seemed at a loss for words.

Charlie found her voice again. She was crying before she even got the words, out... "I went to one of your concerts." She had Lahash's attention now. "I didn't tell your father, but I found out you were performing in Richmond, so I bought a ticket and made an excuse to go spend a weekend there." She paused and studied him, trying to find the word to express what the experience had been like.

He prodded her on. "And did you enjoy it?" he asked with a smirk.

"It was... one of the worst experiences of my life. I couldn't believe what you had become, the things

191

you were saying. I don't know if you did this at all your concerts, or if I just happen to come to the right one to find out what you thought of me, but you held a funeral for me on stage. You read a speech about 'Dear Dying Charlotte' that quite honestly put fear in me, and then you hung me in effigy while singing words I couldn't understand. I felt like I was surrounded by demons. I ran out of the crowd crying, and someone threw beer all over me. That was the last time I tried to find you."

Brent gave her a sympathetic look and then shook his head, remembering how upset he had been after she told him about her experience. "After that, we were ready to give up on you for good. But then Joss called us asking about these magazine articles, and it all came back. She found out about you and wouldn't let it rest especially after she heard you were in bad health. We came because we wanted the opportunity to ask for forgiveness in case something happened to you."

"In case I die, you mean? Would my forgiveness let you live in peace once my body was being devoured by worms? Will your newfound Christian God smile down upon you for this brave move?" he asked sarcastically.

The heartbreak in Brent's face gave way to a new seriousness. He looked directly into Lahash's eyes and spoke without apology or hesitation. "Let me tell you about my Christian God, since you brought Him up. He's a father, like me, and he loves his children. You are one of his children, Lance. I was given stewardship over you as your earthly father, and I blew it. But, I've been given this opportunity to ask your forgiveness and to do whatever is in my power to right the wrongs I've committed against you. God has already forgiven me for my sins of the past. I've been baptized and washed clean, and I felt the relief and the peace that can only come from forgiveness...and from love. Love from our eternal Father. It changed me more than you can imagine, son." Lahash shot him a warning look, and his lips peeled back ready to verbally attack, but Brent cut him off before a complete word was uttered.

"Yes—son! You are my son!" he shouted. "And I'd be a coward if I let the rest of my life or the rest of your life end without telling you I'm sorry!" Then his voice softened, and his throat seemed to close off as he practically whispered the words, "I love you, son." His frame, shook, and the tears returned, but he didn't avert his eyes or attempt to hide it. The tears flowed down his cheek in steady streams and then dropped onto his chest.

The room was quiet and still with every eye on Lahash, whose gaze had been steadily fixed on Brent's until the last words of love were spoken. Then he looked away and stared at nothing in particular. It was as if he'd prepared a counteroffensive to everything but that. A declaration of love was not something he'd ever heard from this man. Fiendish fans had screamed those words at concerts and various other

193

encounters, but it had always felt like nothing more than worship of money or fame to him. Love was an emotion Lahash had very little experience in, and in this moment, he became painfully aware of that. He didn't trust the words, yet there they were, ringing in his ears. And the man who said them stood facing him, overcome with emotion.

Minutes seemed to tick by. Kate was profoundly affected by what she had heard. The feeling emanating from Brent was palpable. She felt out of place saying anything, and so she remained seated, silently watching.

Joss had been hoping Lahash would say something in response to her father, but as more time passed, the less likely it seemed he would. So she cleared her throat and said, "Lance, I can't imagine what's running through your head right now. But I want you to know that this isn't easy for me either. I've been kept from the truth all these years, years that I've spent without my brother who has been out there in the public eye all this time. It's a shame. This has really shaken my foundation, but I for one am glad that Kate's articles were able to bring us all together. I had a very different upbringing than you did, and I know it takes time for wounds to heal, but I hope you're open to reconciliation."

Lahash contemplated his sister for a moment and then asked, "And what would reconciliation look like, huh? You and I come from very different worlds, kitten. Would we all sit around sharing old memories over beers? Like this memory, for example: I was eight years old and I'd been locked out of the house almost the entire day, so Charlotte didn't have to deal with me. I wandered around aimlessly looking for something to do. Some teenage boys saw me and thought they'd have a little fun with me. They gave me a shot of whiskey and told me to run as fast as I could. I'd never had whiskey before, and it made my throat burn and I started coughing. Before I could run off, they set their dog on me. The beast attacked me the whole way home, biting and growling and tearing me up. I was hysterical when I got to the house and started banging on the door. And what did dear old dad do? Oh, he chased the dog off; that he did—the barking was a nuisance. But when I tried to tell him what happened and showed him all the bite marks where blood had been drawn, he smelled the alcohol on my breath and took it out on me. You'd think he'd find the SOBs who did this to his kid, but no not my old man! I got a smack in the back of the head and yelled at for drinking liquor. That was a nice little memory of ours, right old man?" His comment visibly bothered Joss. He took note and continued, cutting off Brent who started to say something. "Yeah, I have plenty of those memories. Shall I continue, or do you want to share one of yours, sis?" Giving voice to the memory seemed to make years of negative feelings come to the surface. Lahash's demeanor had been closed off up to this point, but his retelling the incident seemed to crack open some of the turmoil deep inside of him.

Brent spoke up. "Would it make you feel better if you could hurt me back? I'd let you if I thought it would begin the forgiveness process. But you know as well as I do that hurting people makes us feel worse. If I could go back in time, I'd wrap my arms around that little eight-year-old boy and apologize for not protecting him. I'd bandage his wounds and promise to keep him safe. Then I'd go shoot that animal and take its carcass to the punks who let him loose on you, as a warning. But I can't change the past. All I can do now is..." He trailed off and held his hands open, as if he couldn't find the words to express his desires.

"All we can do now is love you," Charlie broke in. "And be patient. I'll wait till my last breath to hear you say the words 'I forgive you.' I hope that day comes. Until then, we are here for you if you need us." She placed an envelope containing a letter she'd written as a backup in the event they were unable to speak to him today; it also contained all their contact information, so he knew how to reach them if he chose to do so. "I hope your health improves soon. In that letter is my phone number and e-mail. I'd love to get an update on you sometime." With that, Charlie rose to her feet and took Brent's, hand and led him to the door. Before passing through the doorway into the hallway, Brent turned to look at his son. His expression was full of compassion and sorrow. He seemed to be trying to memorize each feature on his son's face. Kate watched his eyes as they traced Lahash's face, and then he turned and left without another word.

Lahash watched them leave, followed by Joss, and then he looked at Kate. Once they were out of earshot, she asked. "Why did you want me to come?"

He laid his head back on the cushion of the chaise and exhaled deeply, closing his eyes. He seemed to be relieved to have the encounter over with.

"No particular reason. Maybe I just wanted you to see the story come full circle. Maybe I wanted you to see that a so-called normal life isn't all it's cracked up to be." His voice was deep and he spoke slowly. He looked defeated. If he'd had something devious planned, it backfired as soon as his dad cried out those first heartbroken words "Oh, my son!"

"Well, what is normal? No family is perfect, you know. I barely speak to my family. Not because of any bad feelings or anything like that. We just aren't close anymore. But the feelings your dad shared today were genuine. That, I know. My own dad has never conveyed so much love to me. For what it's worth, I sympathize with your reluctance to forgive. But I also know that if you do forgive them, it will benefit you probably more than them." Before she had a chance to ask about his health, he abruptly told her to get out. Without waiting for a more forceful dismissal, she left.

As she was pulling out of the driveway, Lahash flung the black silk sheet at the door and then broke down into angry sobs.

8

Several months had passed since the last time Kate had seen Lahash. During that time, she had established a friendship with Joss, and the two of them met occasionally for lunch or dinner, and they spoke on the phone regularly. Unearthing the family skeletons had brought Joss even closer to her parents. She didn't hold any grudges for their past actions. In fact, she admired their humility and the dramatic changes they had made in their lives.

Nobody had heard from Lahash. The only update had come from Oliver, who had e-mailed Kate to tell her that Lahash had canceled the last few tour dates on the doctor's orders. No other performances were scheduled, and his travel was strictly limited. He had a personal nurse who was

199

treating him at home with hemodialysis to improve his kidney function, and a dietician was monitoring his diet to the point of managing everything he put into his body. His physical and emotional condition had worsened due to drug and alcohol withdrawal symptoms, but Oliver was working on him to enter a rehab facility near his home in San Francisco.

At work, Kate was helping to lead the transition from a monthly gossip magazine to a quarterly publication that would shift to provide more in-depth content. The platform would be focused on using the lives of celebrities as the backdrop to focus on more serious topics facing the culture writ large. Celeste had been promoted to a full-time position as her writing assistant, and she was proving to be an invaluable researcher. The innovative overhaul had given Kate a renewed sense of purpose at work. Her personal life was changing as well.

Kate had planned a surprise visit to her parents. Lahash's broken family, and the anguish she had witnessed in his father's face over it all, caused her to reflect on her own family. She didn't want to take those relationships for granted anymore. When she told Markus that she planned to go home for her parents' fortieth anniversary and surprise them with a special dinner, Markus asked if he could come along. They were dating seriously now, and he had a surprise of his own to make.

She arranged for her brother to bring their parents to a small French restaurant where they had been eating dinner when Kate's mother, Meg, had gone into labor with Kate. It was a story she'd heard about many times growing up. Every time they'd driven past it, Meg had pointed out that that was where baby Kate decided to make her entrance into the world. Contractions had set in every three minutes or so, but Meg refused to leave until she'd finished her meal. As she told it, she'd never eaten such a delicious *coq au vin*, and come hell or high water, she'd finish dinner and dessert too! Her dad, Brian, had left a fifty-dollar bill on the table and rushed her to the hospital, arriving just in time to deliver the baby there. Almost thirty-one years later, the place was still in business.

Kate and Markus had arrived early and set a beautiful bouquet of flowers on the table with an envelope containing a pair of George Strait concert tickets as a gift. Her parents had always been country music fans, and she knew they'd love to see a live show. They arrived with Christian and had been happily surprised to meet Kate and Markus there. Two years had passed since she'd last visited them in Arizona. It was a nice reunion. She told them all about her experience with Lahash and the changes at work. They were genuinely interested and told her how proud they were of her. Before the evening came to a close, Markus pulled Brian aside and privately asked him for permission to marry his daughter. It was a nod to tradition, and his way of showing respect to the man who would give her away.

On their last night in Arizona, Markus drove Kate out to a rocky overlook just outside of town. He backed the Ford Escape rental car up, so they could sit in the back cargo area and take in the view. The sky was purple, and the moon was full. The town below them was just beginning to light up for the night, but it was far enough away that they felt removed from civilization. Markus knew that Kate loved to hear him sing in Spanish. She claimed that his voice was better tuned for Spanish, versus when he sang in English, a point he continually tried to disprove by singing along to any song he knew the words to. Tonight, however, he stuck with Spanish. He played a song for her from his iPhone that she'd never heard before. Even though she didn't understand all the words, he sang them to her and the meaning was clear. He loved her. When the song finished, he placed the phone back in his pocket and withdrew a small box. He presented it to her and said simply, "Marry me Kate."

To which she replied, "Gladly!"

He pulled her in for a kiss, placing his hands behind her head and lightly entangling his fingers in the thick strands of hair. She pressed her body into his and savored a long, passionate kiss. It was a glimpse into their wedding night, and she couldn't wait to start planning.

A short time after becoming engaged, wedding plans were in full swing. Kate enlisted Joss's help in choosing a wedding gown. Although she had other close friends whose help she could have employed, Joss's keen eye for the perfect look on any occasion made her the logical choice, and she was happy to oblige. One day while discussing dress details at Joss's office, the topic of wedding guests came up.

"How many people do you plan to invite?" Joss asked.

"We'd like to keep it fairly small. Markus's family is huge, but I've drawn the line at siblings and parents only. He can forget about all those cousins and extended family because I want to have plenty of seats for friends and close work associates. And you're invited, of course. Do you think Lahash would come?" She had asked sarcastically, but it was missed on Joss.

"Really? I was hoping you'd invite him! I've been trying to come up with an excuse to reach out to him. I can't stop thinking about him. My parents keep pestering me for news of him, but I feel like I need a reason to call him. I wouldn't know what to say otherwise."

Kate hadn't seriously thought of inviting Lahash, but mostly because it didn't seem like his cup of tea, even if they had been friends. She wondered how the other guests would react to him. Would he wear his eighteenth-century garb with the top hat? Would she be able to detect the mockery behind his blacked-out eyes? A traditional wedding was just the type of thing he scoffed at and aimed to live in stark contrast to everything it stood for. But she could see that it would mean a lot to Joss, so she said she would get his address from Oliver and send an invitation.

When Markus heard this news, he just stared at Kate in disbelief. Kate added, "And if he comes, I'll probably have to invite Leif. He's a big fan."

"Who's Leif?"

"He's the redheaded barista I told you about."

Markus laughed. "And should we invite the garbage man too? Seriously, it's a no for my cousins, but a yes to Lahash and the redheaded barista from Starbucks. You're something else!"

"Well it would give Joss a reason to try to reconnect with him, and I must admit, I'm a little curious about him too. Hey! Maybe he could be the wedding singer!" she said, trying to contain her laughter.

"Great idea!" Markus said as he threw a shrimp at her. She ducked, but it hit her anyway. It never failed.

They ultimately did mail an invitation to Lahash. Since Joss was not currently dating anyone, she was hoping to attend the event with her brother. Weeks had passed since the invitations had gone out, and thus far, he had not RSVP'd. With the wedding only a month away, Joss got up the nerve to call him. Oliver had given her his private number but had cautioned her to guard it. Lahash was not amenable to sharing his cell phone number with anyone outside of his inner circle. Even giving it to his dietician had been a sore point. After placing several calls, she realized that he was probably screening them, so she left a message for him to call her. He didn't return the call.

About a week later Kate received a voice mail from Joss saying that she would regrettably have to miss the wedding. There was no explanation given, and Kate assumed it had something to do with Lahash. She found out later that Charlie had been in a car accident and was still in critical condition. Joss had flown home to Virginia to be with her parents. It was sad news, of course, but Kate was so distracted with other things that she didn't even try to call Joss back. She'd check back in with her in a few days and see how things were going.

Preparing for the wedding was starting to wear Kate out. Not only did she have plenty of loose ends to tie up without Joss's help, but she and Markus were in the process of buying a home as well. They were hoping to move into a house together right after the honeymoon, but thus far, they had faced obstacle after obstacle. Her landlord was reluctant to let her out of the lease four months early, and twice now they'd made offers on homes that were outbid by other buyers. She hadn't written in her journal for months but decided to make the effort to write tonight because she knew she'd want to remember this hectic transitional period once she was happily on the other side of it.

She put on some loose gym shorts and a T-shirt and began writing about the whole experience, hoping it would help her decompress. The sound of her pen scratching across the paper was interrupted by her phone. Expecting it to be Markus, she jumped up and ran to answer it. However, it was Joss on the other end, and she was crying.

"Kate, my mom's dead." She got the words out and then broke down crying. Kate had never been good at dealing with death. She'd had an aunt pass away once and couldn't bring herself to call her cousins and say how sorry she was. In this case, the words were hard to find because it was so unexpected, and she was surprised Joss would call her just hours afterward. *She must have others who would be better at comforting at a time like this,* Kate thought. But she was genuinely sorry for her friend, and she tried her best to express that.

When Joss had composed herself enough to speak, she said, "I'm sorry to unload this on you. But I don't have anyone else I feel like I can share this with. You met my parents. None of my current friends know them, and I've lost touch with the old friends who knew them well. My dad is here, but he's really a mess and I don't have any other family members around to help with this. Kate, can you come out here and help me plan the funeral? Please?"

Without thinking, Kate said yes. Two days later, she was on a plane headed to Dulles International Airport. She was grateful for the distraction from the wedding. Last-minute details on flower arrangements and catering had been taken over by Deborah Ewing, for which Kate was eternally grateful. Markus was left in charge of honeymoon plans.

Driving through the Virginia countryside was a new experience for Kate. The freeways were lined with walls of green foliage, and there were sprawling farms and beautiful estates all throughout Loudoun County. Joss parents lived in a small rural town called Waterford. Their home had been built in the late 1800s and was situated on eight acres of lush green land. The stone walls and black shutters had all the colonial-style charm. Kate was offered the guest bedroom upstairs. From the bedroom window, she could see the rolling hills in the distance that looked blue. There were cows out to pasture in a field with an old red barn on it that looked as though it had come from another era.

There was a sadness that permeated the whole place. Brent would spend most of his time sitting in the rocker on the front porch. He seldom spoke and only picked at the food Joss would bring him. Joss had been so relieved at Kate's arrival. They immediately made arrangements for the funeral. It was to be held two days from now at a funeral home in Leesburg. It was strange to go from choosing flower arrangements for a wedding to choosing

207

flowers for a funeral almost overnight. Joss had managed to get in touch with all the family she knew of, including her Aunt Beth, whom she'd only met once before. She and Kate had both tried to reach Lahash, but to no avail. Oliver received the news and offered his condolences. He and Markus had both sent flowers to the house as well.

On the day of the funeral, there was a light rain falling. Brent was waiting in the car for the two women at 9:00 a.m. sharp. They rode together to Leesburg but spoke very little. Despite the occasion, Kate couldn't help notice how nicely put together Joss looked. She wore a simple black dress that had an empire waist and capped sleeves; it was fitted and came down just passed her knees. Her necklace was comprised of a thin silver chain with a black pearl pendant enclosed in a silver circle. She also wore black pearl earrings that were nicely on display with her hair pinned up into a wispy knot. The simple elegance of her appearance could have been fit for the symphony or some other preferable outing. Yet paired with the somberness of her demeanor, it was a respectful tribute to the deceased.

When they arrived at the funeral home, the director met them at the door and ushered them into a small chapel where the memorial service would be held. The casket, which remained closed, was placed to the left side of the pulpit. It was a rich-brown wood and was draped in bunches of white lilies and purple lilacs. As Kate was not family, she chose a seat near the back. She watched people filing in, quietly greeting each other and sharing tearful hugs. For some reason, she kept expecting to see Lahash cross the threshold in his black tailcoat, but instead, the attendees were mostly neighbors and church friends.

About ten minutes into the services, a woman with short graying hair slipped into the chapel and quietly took a seat on the pew across the aisle from Kate. She wore a black broomstick-style skirt with folds of crinkled material, and a charcoal-gray sweater. Her face wore the look of a tough life. There were deep frown lines etched into her countenance that were deeper than the rest of the wrinkles. Her eyes conveyed a mixture of sadness and anger, and they remained fixed on the casket. Kate guessed that she was Aunt Beth, the woman who had unsuccessfully tried to raise Lahash. Kate's gaze kept wandering back to this woman as several speakers stood at the pulpit telling fond memories of Charlie. She noted that nobody mentioned Charlie's son, even though most of them made reference to Joss in some way or another. For her part, the woman remained stoic.

The service closed with a rendering of "Amazing Grace," sung by a tall, wiry man with a deep, grainy, voice. It was beautiful. Then the hearse led the funeral procession on a slow, winding ride through the green hills to an ancient looking cemetery that was encircled by a crumbling stone wall. It was only about an acre of land, and scanning the whole thing, you'd see a smattering of small Confederate and American flags posted in front of headstones. Having grown up in the West, Kate was struck by the placing of Confederate flags even today.

The air was wet and heavy with the continuous drizzle of rain. The pallbearers carried the casket across the grass and placed it in front of the freshly dug hole in the ground, while everyone else clustered close together under umbrellas. Joss and Brent stood together under a large black umbrella with their arms locked. Both were crying. A religious man in a dark suit and tie, presumably a leader from their church, gave some remarks at the gravesite. He spoke optimistically of reuniting with family members in the afterlife and of eternal peace.

All of a sudden, the woman whom Kate presumed was Beth gasped and stepped away from the group. She looked surprised and kept taking slow step farther away, her eyes concentrating on something—no, someone—at the far end of the cemetery boundaries. Kate followed her gaze and noticed a tall black figure in the distance. Her disruption caused a momentary pause in the man's eloquent speech, but after a quick look around, he picked up where he left off. The old woman began walking toward the figure in the distance, and then she ran, stumbling several times. Her running was more like frantic walking, but there was urgency in her movement. The figure remained in place. When she reached the man, Kate could tell she threw her arms around him, but it was not reciprocated. *He came,* thought Kate.

Joss and Brent were utterly engrossed in what was being said and hadn't noticed what was happening at the other end of the cemetery. Kate couldn't help herself. She started walking in the direction of the two people, who were still conversing. As she got closer, she could hear the woman crying, saying, "Lance, answer me!" He wasn't looking at her; rather, he watched Kate approach.

Lahash was dressed in black from head to foot. He wasn't wearing the top hat or any of the gothic makeup or freaky contact lenses. His hair was brushed back into a neat ponytail, which was dripping wet from the rain. His arms were crossed in front of his chest, and his nails were painted black. He leaned casually against a tall headstone that bore a stone cross.

"Lahash," said Kate, "I didn't think you would come."

"Kate," was all he said.

The old woman turned to Kate and asked in an irritated voice, "Who are you?'

"I'm sorry for interrupting. My name is Kate Owens. I've done some work with Lahash," she said as she nodded toward him. Then she attempted to shake hands, but the woman just stood there.

211

"Stop calling him that! His name is Lance."

"This is my charming Aunt Beth," said Lahash sarcastically.

Beth glared at him, and then the tears welled up again. She wiped her face and sniffed angrily. Ignoring Kate's presence, she resumed talking to Lahash. "I loved you like a son, you know! Why didn't you tell me you were leaving? Why didn't you ever come back?" Her voice was strong, but it kept breaking because she was overcome with emotions.

Finally, he looked at her, and there was a hint of pity in his eyes as he studied the old woman. After a long pause, he said, "I left because of music, not because of you. And I never came back because I didn't need to. You were better off without me anyway."

Her voice tendered as she responded, "Maybe you were better off without me, but I wasn't. I needed you. You gave my life purpose, even when you made me so mad I wanted to ring your neck!" He smirked. "It's the truth. You never would listen to anything that was good for you."

Kate could tell that Beth's words had touched him. All three of them looked on at the group of people who were steadily leaving the gravesite. Little by little, they got in their cars and drove away. Joss had noticed Kate leave, but she refrained from following her until the casket had been lowered into the ground and people started leaving. Once that happened, she left Brent alone and made her way over to where the three stood.

The clouds were growing darker, and the rain picked up. When Joss reached them, she stopped in front of Lahash and just stood there without saying anything. Her tears mingled with the raindrops that streamed down her face. They were all getting soaked. Kate gave her a hug and said, "I'll meet you at the car." Stubbornly, Beth stayed there.

Over the sound of the rain, she heard Joss thank Lahash for coming. Then she turned around and glanced back just in time to see him step toward his sister and hug her. Beth stood there awkwardly staring at the mud on her shoes.

Kate made her way to the car and put in a call to Markus. She related the day's events to him and then listened to his updates on the honeymoon plans. As they spoke, she watched Brent drop a single red rose into the hole where the casket lay. After a few minutes, Beth went over to where he stood and remained by his side until Joss and Lahash joined them. The four of them stood together for a few minutes. If they were talking, Kate couldn't tell. Then she hung up the phone just as Joss climbed into the car. Beth returned to her car and drove away.

Brent and his son stood together over Charlie's grave. Nobody but the two of them heard the words that were uttered.

9

$\mathcal{T}$he night air was cool and breezy. The waning moon shed just enough light for Kate to admire the newly planted flower garden near her back patio. The scent of flowers and fresh dirt wafted past her and took her mind back three months to the funeral. Thinking of all that had transpired since then reminded her that she hadn't had time to write in her journal for a while. Some of the most significant events in her life yet, and probably to come, had happened during the past three months, and she wanted to record it all. She rose from the Adirondack chair and gathered her things. She'd been reading a new book and doing research on her iPad intermittently, until it had grown too dark to read. The peach cobbler sat on the side table half eaten.

Markus was already in bed asleep when she entered their bedroom to collect her journal and the same fountain pen that had written every word in it since the beginning. She admired him for a moment as he snored softly and then bent over and kissed him on the cheek. Then she turned off every light on her way to the living room except for the oiled bronze floor lamp which stood next to the reclining chair. She settled down into the squishy leather chair, let her ponytail out, and propped her feet up. Taking pen to paper, she wrote,

Dear Journal,

I have been remiss in keeping you informed of life's happening lately, and for that, I will go to bed late tonight in order to make up for it. I am a changed woman since the last time I wrote. Not only has my name and marital status changed, but I've been changed on the inside as well. Let's start with my name change, and then I'll delve into how my heart has been changed.

My name is now Kate Barranco, and I wear it proudly. I married my neighbor, Markus Barranco, whom I have written of previously. He proposed to me under the starlit desert sky of Arizona, and we wed under the brilliant blue sky of our home state of California. October 17 will forever mark the anniversary of our new life together. Jed and Deborah hosted the wedding at their home, which was a late change. Originally, we'd wanted to have the wedding at a barn in wine country, but upon hearing that we would not purchasing wine, they informed us that there would be an additional 20 percent surcharge. It was disappointing, but it worked out better in the end. Having it at a private home saved us enough money to splurge on our honeymoon. I'll get back to that in a minute.

All the planning that caused me so much stress during the previous months came together perfectly. The surface of the pool was covered in pink and yellow rose petals, with large flower arrangements posted on pedestals at the four corners. Folding chairs had been arranged on one side of the lawn for the ceremony, and tables were arranged on the other side for the hors d'oeuvres and cake. And what delicious food it was! Our cake mirrored the pool with pink and yellow petals flowing down and around the sides of each tier. The tiny bride and groom that were placed on top were sporting running shoes under their wedding attire, which was perfect for us. Deb had found them at some bridal boutique, and they even looked like us.

My father walked me down the aisle. We don't talk often, so it was strange to ask him for the favor. But he was happy to do it, and I dare say, we bonded over the experience. He and

Mom never did the traditional thing; they eloped off to Santa Fe when they got married, and so this was his first walk down the wedding aisle. Just before we took our first step, he whispered that he was nervous and to catch him if he tripped or stumbled. There were no tears when he handed me over to Markus, just happiness. The tears, surprisingly, came from Jed.

After the 'I dos,' Markus ignored my previous instructions to perform a simple kiss (I'm uncomfortable with PDA), and he planted a full mouthed, long, wet one, holding me so tight I was unable to break away (nor did I want to). Amazingly, my lipstick stayed in place, thanks to Joss's makeup expert who is a miracle worker. Coincidentally, my favorite picture, of the day was the one of us locked in a kiss at the altar with his hands tightly wrapped around my waist.

The wedding guests were an oddball collection of family from both sides, colleagues, friends, and a few surprises. No, in case you were wondering, Lahash—correction: Lance— did not come. He did, however, send a gift. But I get ahead of myself. The attendee whose presence most surprised me was Jill. Did I invite the receptionist who drives me batty? Of course not, but she came as a date with an invited guest. Leif, of all people! I told him he shouldn't date another redhead, but his braids must have blocked that out. If I had to guess how that arrangement happened, I'd have to say that she must have heard about the wedding and inquired around about who was going. And Leif was her mark. She probably dropped hints, knowing that he'd given her a second look that day at the office. And just like that, she's there schmoozing with the other guests and flipping her red hair around. I can't say I'm mad about it though; Leif looked like a puppy out for its first walk. "Happy, happy, happy!" as Phil Robertson would say. Mozzella was there too, and she brought her boyfriend. He's white. Not that that matters, but it kind of surprised me that she would date a white guy. I can see why she likes him though. He's a football player, tall, charming, and nice as can be. His Southern manners were straight out of the most refined cotillion.

The gift Lance sent was interesting, to say the least. Before I divulge what it was, I have to back up in my story in order for you to understand the significance of it. Let me take you back to a rain-soaked Virginia cemetery. I was sitting in the car watching with rapt attention as Lahash and his father stood at Charlie's grave. The older man's head was bowed, never turning to look at his estranged son, even in this hour of grief and loss. For a long time, the son stood just a few feet away, staring into the hole where his mother lay. Their backs were turned to me, so I had no idea if they were speaking to each other or not. After a while, Brent lifted his head and looked up toward the sky. As he did so, Lahash turned to him, unfolded his arms, and wrapped them around his father, who looked startled, not just at the unlikely embrace but by the mere presence. It was as if Brent hadn't even realized Lahash had been there standing next to him.

It wasn't until later that evening that I heard what happened. Back at the house, Brent's demeanor had completely changed. Where before he was solemn, and grief stricken, afterward, he was lighter somehow and smiled easily. He ate his entire dinner and did it joyfully. Joss commented how strange his behavior was, and he said if you knew what happened that afternoon, you'd understand. I still don't quite understand, even after the explanation, but either way, it was a small miracle. Brent said that he'd waited until everyone walked away so he could have one last "conversation" with Charlie. He was so wrapped up in his own thoughts and feelings that he barely registered it when people came and stood at his side. After Joss and Beth left for their cars, Brent thought he was alone again. He'd had no inclination that Lahash had even come to the internment, let alone that he was standing just a few feet away listening to the words that Brent expressed in impassioned prayer. Brent did not relate the words of the prayer, only that he poured his heart and soul out. After saying "Amen," he looked up toward heaven to see if he could see her face one last time. As he did so, a pair of arms wrapped around him and startled him "out of his skin" as he said. He stood there dumbfounded as Lance held him in a tight hug and barely audible over the rain said, "I forgive you. And I'm sorry too."

I cried that night. That was an incredible human moment, and it wasn't even mind. Although, I think I can claim a tiny part of it. Remembering back to the first time I attended church with Markus, I thought about how I was so eager to do something good for someone else. I was looking for a "service project" that would help me feel the way I felt that night, only I couldn't have expressed that then because I had no idea how incredibly tangible the feelings of love and forgiveness can be. Markus was right when he said that I should wait for the opportunity to find me, one that only I could fulfill. I truly believe that if I had never done those interviews, these two men would never have forgiven each other. Not only that, but they never would have spoken at all. And what a tragedy to think that it was there all along, those feelings of betrayal and hurt, just wanting to be released. Here were two souls so battered and beaten that they could have gone all their earthly lives never seeking each other out, only to die carrying that burden. I am blessed to have served a purpose in healing a family.

Before leaving Virginia, I removed one of my Venice beads from the pouch in my purse and left it on Brent's desk with a note that read, "Thank you for teaching me about humility and forgiveness. It will serve me well in my upcoming marriage. This bead has traveled to you all the way from Venice to remind you that goodness always triumphs over darkness."

That brings me back to Lance. He has dropped his stage name and dismantled the band. He checked himself into rehab, but his health issues continue to be a struggle. As a show of "good faith" that he will never return to that life even if he "remains a blemish on the edge of society" as he says, he gave us the black RV he toured in as a wedding present. Oliver drove it to the ceremony with a giant purple bow on it. And in true Lahash fashion, for it was a remnant of his former persona, he littered the bed with condoms and porn movies (which were quickly thrown in the trash). Markus was thrilled at the thought of road tripping in such luxury, although he scoured it with disinfectant and is still slightly leery of sleeping in that bed, given its previous occupant.

For my part, I mailed him a gift in return. Being the self-taught, educated man that he is, who reads voraciously, I mailed him the book

Jesus the Christ by James Talmage, and of course, a trashy novel, just to make him feel normal. And included in the package was another one of my Venice beads. I wrapped it in a torn-out page of *What Pops*; it was the page containing my first interview with him, and I highlighted the section that challenged him to be a true rarity and change his life. Then beneath it, I wrote, "I win."

My gift was not intended to be snarky. In the end, he won too. He has changed course. It will not be easy for him, and he will probably suffer for a while as he reconciles his identity. There are many aspects of his past that will always haunt him, and like bony fingers from the past, those skeletons will surely claw at him; the Demon Lahash will whisper in his ear sweet enticing promises of fame and fortune, if only he would...(fill in the blank). But he's been there before, and he knows all the trappings of those promises, and for now anyway, he has chosen the path least traveled. Time will tell if he is a true rarity. I will cheer him on privately, and maybe one day, I'll write his story.

I did promise to write about my honeymoon, but on second thought, I think I'll keep that story all to myself.

4-U-Nique Publishing

Read excerpts, get exclusive inside looks at exciting new titles and authors, find tour schedules and enter contests.

www.4-U-NiquePublishing.com

Need help publishing your masterpiece? We are happy to help.

Email us at info@4-U-NiquePublishing.com